BOTLHODI
The Abomination
Translated with a Critical Introduction
By Keith Robert Phetlhe

A Postcolonial Setswana Novel by
T.J. Pheto

Langaa Research & Publishing CIG
Mankon, Bamenda

Publisher:
Langaa RPCIG
Langaa Research & Publishing Common Initiative Group
P.O. Box 902 Mankon
Bamenda
North West Region
Cameroon
Langaagrp@gmail.com
www.langaa-rpcig.net

Distributed in and outside N. America by African Books Collective
orders@africanbookscollective.com
www.africanbookcollective.com

ISBN-10: 9956-550-55-8

ISBN-13: 978-9956-550-55-5

© T.J. Pheto 2019

'We went to their church. Mubia, in white robes, opened the Bible. He said: Let us kneel down to pray. We knelt down. Mubia said: Let us shut our eyes. We did. You know, his remained open so that he could read the word. When we opened our eyes, our land was gone and the sword of flames stood on guard. As for Mubia, he went on reading the word, beseeching us to lay our treasures in heaven where no moth would corrupt them. But he laid his on earth, our earth.'

Ngugi wa Thiong'o, *A Grain of Wheat*

I dedicate this work to the author of the Setswana novel T.J Pheto for being among the first writers to write this fiction of resistance that chronicles Botswana's anti-colonial crisis. I also thank him for granting me permission to translate this work into English.

This novel is a remarkable literary response to British colonial presence and its aftermath on Bakwena of Molepolole in Botswana. Also, to Prof. Ngugi wa Thiong'o who did the same in East Africa.

Tiroentle Bafana Pheto

Table of Contents

Acknowledgements

I would like to give my sincere thanks to all those who made this work possible. First and foremost, I thank the author, Tiroentle Bafana Pheto, for giving me a very warm welcome during my unannounced visit to Molepolole and for granting me a permission to translate his novel into English. I acknowledge Pula Press for publishing this novel in Setswana in 1985. And to my friend Dr. Joel Magogwe who drove with me to Molepolole to Rre Pheto's house. Although he was not expecting us, he gave us his time. My family back home in Botswana who went through a long period of an absent sibling, father, and uncle. I say a special thank you to my beloved daughter Maya who had been born a few months before I left on my self-imposed academic exile. And to you Annah Diundu my love, thank you for taking care of my daughter and loving me unconditionally; I love you.

In a long list of mentors and friends, I start by thanking Professor Ghirmai Negash for offering direction and advice throughout; and his expertise and criticism which has always challenged me to the limits but also made me a better researcher and translator. I also thank him for helping me regain confidence in postcolonial African literatures. At the University of Botswana's African Languages & Literature, I thank Drs. R. Nhlekisana and P. Seloma for believing in me. I also thank the Government of Botswana and African Studies Program at Ohio University for sponsoring my studies. While I cannot thank and mention all individuals involved in the project by name, I would like also to thank Dr. Steve Howard, formerly the Director of Center for International Studies who directed the African Studies Program for almost three decades. And to Bose Maposa, the assistant director of African Studies Program as well as Mr. Master Baipidi of the Embassy of Botswana to the US in Washington D.C. I say thank you for your valuable advice and support. Pula! I also would like to thanks my colleagues at Ohio University, especially Lassane Ouedraogo, James Fisher and Spencer Cappelli.

I am grateful to David Lawrence for the cover design.

By drawing from the historical tradition and the imposition of Christianity in Botswana during British colonialism Botlhodi-The Abomination leaves readers with more questions than answers. These two aspects; tradition and religion combine to form a plethora of doubt within the social institutions known to have previously held Bakwena ethnic group in unison. As an ethnic group that was once held together by its social norms, values and a common way of life, the Bakwena find themselves divided by a foreign religion and a colonial government that disregards the bogosi institution. The new religion, pioneered by British missionaries parades with only one serious objective: to despise traditional ways of the Bakwena, the people whose totem is a crocodile. The claim that African tradition is nothing but a litany of barbaric deeds and witchcraft practiced by a people who require 'civilization' is used by the colonial missionaries who strategically use religion as a weapon to divide and conquer. In addition, the colonial government does not recognize the system of Bogosi despite its significance to the people of Kweneng as a whole. The paramount chief of Bakwena gets converted to Christianity and because of this every villager is expected to be part of the church led by a white missionary, who plays the role of both a medical doctor and a pastor in the novel. However, this change comes with a price of cohesion and force, sometimes death from unbearable persecution for the villagers who refuse to comply and compromise their traditional principles. As a result, the Morafe of Bakwena is brutally divided, both socially and ideologically as the colonialists influence their traditional leadership to turn things upside down through indoctrination. The novelist uses dark images, symbols and metaphors to tie the entire narrative together in his questioning of colonialism.

Pheto questions the project of colonialism in Botswana and juxtaposes it with the challenges it poses: for example it causes religious assimilation in the sense that it expects the locals to abandon their beliefs for the colonizer's. Through this novel, Pheto transcends as one of the few writers of Setswana literature who writes back to the empire in his native Setswana, therefore compelling many people whose identity was attacked and compromised by the colonial predicament. Botlhodi-The Abomination therefore counts among the first remarkable literary responses to colonialism in Botswana. Pheto's work demonstrates how early Christianity during colonial time should be held responsible for racism, discrimination and prejudices that the Bakwena find themselves grappling with. When Bakwena combine Christianity with traditional beliefs as their preferred way of worship they are met with abject persecution. Clearly, their effort to interpret biblical doctrines against tradition is rejected and disqualified on racial grounds. The reason for this is very simple and obvious—there is a belief that there is no Church that can exist without a British White man as a pastor and Kgosi as a member.

Pheto meticulously adopts the use of humorous language to address issues of racism and racial profiling stereotypes brought by the colonizers to the traditional society. However, some of the humor may be lost, due to translation into another language that may likely compromise organic exoticness and quality of the Tswana humor. For example, we note that some characters in the novel are amused but at the same time perplexed and disgusted by examples of modernity, such as having a toilet in the same house where people live. Beer, although it is habitually consumed and loved is compared with human urine in a glass. Characters are depicted as experiencing a change for the first time, so in the process they get shocked and express this in their daily conversations. To the Bakwena people, this is tantamount to insanity! The novelist carefully constructs his characters in a way that allows for a juxtaposition between the themes of modernity versus tradition. Pheto's literary offering tells a story about the history of Bakwena in a fictitious style that pays attention to specific cultural details. By defying the mainstream style of writing that is based on the canons, the novel evokes a strong application of African fiction writing in the quality of its narratology. In the midst of persecution, Bakwena who have formed their own church and a few traditionalists who evidently resist the colonial rule have only tradition to use as their weapon hence they may appear weak yet they keep fighting. It is not an easy walk of life, but it is one of a kind that is marked by a sea of screams from the oppressed other, whether one is a king, a conscript, or a commoner.

Keith Robert Phetlhe, Ph.D Canditate, African Literature & Film Studies Interdisciplinary Arts, is a poet, teacher, writer and, cultural enthusiast from Botswana. He holds a BA in African Languages & Literature and English Studies from the University of Botswana. In addition, he holds a Postgraduate Diploma in Education from the same university, where he trained as teacher of Setswana language and English. Phetlhe has also received a Master of Arts in African Studies, with special focus on African Literature, where his research interests are Postcolonial Literature and Literary Translation at Ohio University in Athens. He was the instructor for Setswana at Ohio University in the African Studies Program. Currently, Keith Phetlhe is the recipient of the Comparative Arts Scholarship from College of Fine Arts in the School of Interdisciplinary Arts. He pursues a Ph.D in African Literature with a minor in Film Studies where he teaches an Introduction to the Arts: African Literature. Phetlhe's research interests are in literary arts in African languages, Translation Studies and Criticism, Postcolonial Studies and Comparative Literature.

The Situation of Translation in Botswana Literature Written in Setswana Language: Criticism and Practice

The role of translation in the development and transformation of various aspects of both traditional and modern Botswana literature cannot be overlooked. This is not only because of its significance in defining and describing the different categories of the literature but also due to fact that translation has opened paths that make it possible to theorize and critique Setswana literature in the context of translation studies. Translation in Setswana literature applies to a vast volume of works encompassing the written and oral genres. This project aims to explore the perspectives and arguments that have been submitted by various translators and authors with respect to translation in Setswana literature in general. While recognizing that, at different historical periods, translation as a process has patently transpired in other local languages spoken in Botswana in a similar fashion, the present study exclusively focuses on the literary production in the Setswana language. In addition to being the common parlance, Setswana boasts a sizeable body of literature, some of which have been translated into European languages, mainly English. The examples of works that are considered for description and critique in this study are drawn from the oral and written traditions of Setswana literature. These include oral poetry, oral narratives such as proverbs and folktales, written poetry, novels, and plays. Based on the critical discussion of these works, the study also aims to investigate the impact of translation on the formation and transformation of these genres that constitute the body of Setswana literature. This research project builds on few existing translation studies on Botswana literature. But, unlike most of the existing studies, it also goes beyond those studies in that it acknowledges and contextualizes the work of translation not merely as a new literary invention in the language but also in its instrumental function in enhancing and diversifying the trajectories of Setswana literature as a whole.

I

Since the colonization of African societies in the 1880s, literary critics and historians have been engaged in a continued and heated debate about what accurately represents African literature. This is due to complex factors, but primarily due to: 1) the absence of uniformity of the different literary traditions associated with the multiple languages and cultures in the continent, and 2) the tendency of critics who attempted to define African literatures based on Western notions. Despite the impositions, the result was that traditional literature in Africa has continued to assume and maintain its existence and identity in various forms and mediums. Translation was one of these important mediums.

In Setswana, both oral and written literary traditions have long existed in the form of oral poetry and narratives (proverbs and folktales), written poetry, novels, and plays. In this process, Botswana literary works have also been translated into other languages mainly English. This study primarily aims to investigate the impact of translation on the formation and transformation of these genres that constitute the body of Setswana literature. The project further builds on few existing translation studies on Botswana literature. However, unlike most of the existing studies, it goes beyond those studies in that it sees the role of translation in Setswana literature not merely as a new literary invention in the language but also as having instrumental function in enhancing and diversifying the historical development of Setswana literature as a whole.

Translation as a new literary invention in Setswana has affected or impacted both the written and oral forms of Setswana literature in several ways. One significant area in which the impact of translation is evident is demonstrated in the way previously recorded oral poetry was transcribed from the oral to its written form. In many instances, before they were available for translation, oral poems had to be first written down, that is, be transcribed into a written text of Setswana orthography. This was necessary not only to facilitate the logistics of translation but importantly so in order to create a written physical and visual equivalent with the English language into which they were translated. This means that the process of translation of any given oral text required a complex procedure involving double translations: from oral to written Setswana, and from written Setswana into English. The procedure of double translation, which often was the norm with translators, in turn, produced the effect that a textual interplay came into being between the original language (written Setswana) and the target language (written English). Concretely, the result of this method of transcribing and translating is seen in many publications such as Schapera, Plaatjie, and Raditladi. Isaac Schapera in his book, Praise-poems of Tswana Chiefs, highlights these steps and procedure of translation when he discusses his methodology. He underscores that:

> None of the texts was recorded by myself. They were all specifically written for me by teachers or other literate Tswana: occasionally by the composer's dictation, from the dictation of other men familiar with the poems, and, now and then, from personal knowledge; and of many, notably Kgatla and Ngwato, I have two or more independent versions. (39)

Another important observation that can be made about translation from Setswana into English pertains to the texts' suitability for translation and the way translation work was debated on by critics in the Botswana context. Fundamentally, critics were divided along three lines of arguments. There were those who were skeptical of the idea of translation, claiming that the art foreignized Botswana culture and literature (Shole 51-55). There were others, while accepting the idea of translation, showed reservations about the translatability of some Setswana ideas and expressions into English (Seboni 2011: Intro). A third group argued that, as a language, Setswana had the vitality to express human values that can be translated into any other language (Schalkwyk and Lapula 10, Makutoane and Naude 79).

At this initial point, I want to dwell on the idea of translation as a process, and as a literary invention that has influenced Setswana literature in its history. Arguably, and despite the criticisms, translation is deemed relevant for a critical inquiry such as this because it opens the opportunities for exploring the role of translation in Setswana literature, as in any other literatures which have translation work as an integral part of their historical development and literary criticism. From a broader perspective, translation studies is a very important area in comparative studies of literature, particularly those representing postcolonial settings. In the context of Botswana, the importance of translation is even more paramount, given the fact that novels such as Chinua Achebe's Things Fall Apart are read and discussed in the country in Setswana language. From the perspective of translation studies, reading Things Fall Apart in Setswana is an exciting development. First, it shows the possibility of translation within African languages. Second, it offers a model of comparison about how Setswana novels can be translated into English and or other African languages and attain wider readership thus making it possible to study Setswana literature as part of world or global literatures. Thirdly, it provides a vital framework to amplify the discussion on translation in Botswana by focusing on this single work. Similar arguments apply to the translation discussed in this research, including Schapera, translator of *Praise-poems of Tswana Chiefs*, Raditladi's *Dintshontsho tsa Lorato*, and Thedi's translation of Bessie Head's *When Rain Clouds Gather.*

What follows is a brief outline of this critical assessment of the situation of translation studies and its relationship with Setswana literature. In the first section, a detailed background of translation and its relationship with Setswana literature is provided. In this section, a first attempt to conceptually define Setswana literature is made. Since a holistic definition of what Setswana literature constitutes has never been given, this part will necessarily be exploratory and hypothetical. It will be followed by a list of objectives and research questions. Consequently, a justification for this study will be provided explaining the necessity and rationale of this investigation. The importance of researching African language literatures, such as Setswana, is highlighted. A discussion on some theories of translations follows. The section concludes with a discussion of the critical literature on translation as viewed by published commentators and theorists of Setswana orature and literature. As per the aims on the criticality of this subject, I put emphasis on the following four specific objectives: first, this research seeks to describe the extent to which translation has been an integral component of Setswana literature. Second, it aims to examine the statements made by critics about Setswana translations. Third, it aspires to contribute to the discussion on translation by analyzing specific samples of translation. Four, it sets to appreciate the instrumental function of translation in enhancing and diversifying the trajectories of Setswana literature as a whole.

Why is Studying Translation Important in Relation to Setswana Literature?

Despite its potential to expand the thematic scope of Setswana literature, there has been very little work on literary translation on Setswana literature. It continues to be largely neglected by critics, and even translators. Comparatively, the focus of Botswana literary critics is, unfortunately, on works that are written in the English language. While understanding the complex forces at play that privilege Anglophone literatures in the country, this research attempts to break that dichotomy between the equally important literatures in Botswana namely European language and the African language literatures. In other words, this project is built on the presumption that Setswana indigenous literatures deserve equal critical attention with the predominant postcolonial Europhonic literatures, which while assuming a center stage have also contributed to the historical invisibility and marginalization of Setswana language literary productions. This position does not stand on its own, but rather underscores what some Setswana literary figures have recognized in their writings. For example, Shole, amplifying the same point, observes that: "not much attention has been given to literary translations in Setswana, either as translations or works of art on their own, despite the role they have played" (Shole 51). If such gaps are addressed through developing this area of inquiry, there is a possibility that the outcome is that more texts and reviews pertaining to Setswana literature are produced such that the primary literary production and translation work become central, rather than peripheral to the study of Botswana literature as an academic discipline. From an academic point of view, it is also this unique concern to empower and recognize the significance of Setswana literature in Botswana and its translations that make this study unique in its purpose and scope. No work that recognizes and analyzes the historical and critical role of translation in Setswana literature has been done before.

II

The section explores translation in terms of how it is mapped into the literary development of Setswana literature in many respects. It first considers the definition as a significant part of the discourse without which this discussion would be incomplete. The next important consideration focuses exclusively on the background of translation in Botswana context, and for this I utilize a more generalized approach that looks into how much has been written about translation in Botswana since colonial period and beyond. Hence, a brief discussion of translation under classifications of religion, fictionality and research is considered.

What is Setswana Literature?

For the purposes of this critical introduction Setswana literature is broadly defined to constitute any literary work that has its oral and written origins in all parts of Southern Africa where Setswana is predominantly spoken as a native language. Those countries include: Botswana, South Africa, Namibia and Zimbabwe. In the Botswana context, there is historical and literary evidence that Setswana literature is a living integral part of the society's culture. Setswana literature is part of the country's school curriculum, printed works are published, reviewed and read by the literary community, while performances of oral poetry and narratives are ubiquitous especially in the rural areas. Despite the dominance of English language literature, Batswana view their indigenous literature as a significant force in the formation of their cultural identity. As creative art, it assumes the important function of creating and enhancing aesthetic experience and general cultural awareness, and fostering communal cohesion. With regards to the nature of Setswana literature, social relevance, fictionality and imagination are viewed as its inherent elements that define its quality. Social or cultural relevance in Setswana literature, like in all African literatures, is dependent on notions of space and time. This means that Setswana literature is shaped by historical currents, while sometimes also contributing to those developments.

In *A History of Tigrinya Literature* (2010), Ghirmai Negash attests to this claim when defining Tigrinya literature when he makes the following crucial statement which in principle applies to African literature in its entirety. He writes that: "'literature is a relative, time and place bound concept, which, therefore, is always subject to change and to being redefined within the course of its own history" (Negash 76). From this definition we gather that to defining African literature is a complex undertaking which forces us to think about the cultural contexts, relativity dynamism that cannot be overlooked when defining. In *Praise Poems of Tswana Chiefs*, Isaac Schapera quotes Lestrade making a similar assertion which compares with Negash's way of define. However, Lestrade focuses on poetry as an example of literature among the Tswana people whom he had studied as an anthropologist. Lestrade states that, among the Tswana people, "[These] compositions are regarded by the Bantu themselves as the highest products of their literary art," which has developed across history and geographies creating different genres of literature when discussing the manner in which Batswana perceived their oral literary traditions (Lestrade qtd. in Schapera 2).

In the Setswana language, the term literature has been translated as padi, which is the derivative of the verb bala or to read. In this sense, the term padi as a label thus privileges written Setswana literature over the oral form. In order to avoid this dichotomy inherent in the word padi, in this project I have decided to use the English term "literature" to refer to both Setswana written and oral forms. Lestrade gives a vivid yet limited description of 'orality' and 'performance' as constituting an important part of this form of literature. He does this by observing that "they are a type of intermediate composition between the pure, mainly narrative epic, and the pure, mainly apostrophic ode, being a combination of exclamatory narration and laudatory apostrophizing" (Lestrade qtd. in Schapera 2). To help us define Setswana literature as a composite of African literature, the critic, Isidore Okpewho, that specializes in oral literature underlines in his African Oral Literature that it would be illogical to use a definition that only fits into the Western mainstream way of defining, which is basically "creative texts that appeal to our imagination or our emotions" (4). This way of definiing immediately disqualifies significant elements of orature that should be a part of defining Setswana literature. Therefore, the term padi does not hold. However, Okpewho offers a suggestion that if we are to define, it is crucial that out way of defining accommodates both the oral and the written literary forms in which case oral literature, according to Okpewho, would mean "literature delivered by word of mouth...thereby emphasizing on the oral character of the literature" (4-5).

Okpewho, Lestrade, and Negash present interesting perspectives which place emphasis on the fact that literature should be defined by the people whose culture significantly emulate how they perceive it, and not necessarily on the basis of foreign, western impositions which have historically, and continually, influenced structure and form of literature. Due to the oral culture of its people, it is a challenge to draw conclusions based on exact historical origins of oral aspects of Setswana literature which date back to the prehistoric era. Setswana literature thus constitutes Botswana literature, which is a conceptual embodiment of all forms of literatures or literary works that were written, perceived orally, documented, and published in Botswana, and it should be about Botswana by the native speakers of the language. However, Botswana presents a complex dichotomy, as noted linguists such as Herman Batibo draw our attention to over 28 languages which are spoken in the country but are familiar with Setswana language and culture. However, historically it remains a fact that there have been non-native speakers of this language who learned it for purposes of conducting research and executing duties as colonial administrators during the time when Botswana was still a British 'protectorate'. At that point, colonial missionaries who sought to spread Christianity among the natives found exploitation of the language to be extremely pivotal in carrying out their mission.

A similar approach used by Ghirmai Negash in defining Tigrinya literature in A History of Tigrinya Literature in Eritrea: the Oral and the Written is closely followed in constructing the definition of Setswana literature. Tigrinya Literature is defined on the basis of its origins and important historical periods. While acknowledging the challenge that comes with any attempt to define literature as a whole, Negash notes that,

> At the general level, however, in so far as my assumption and utilization of the term 'Tigrinya literature' in this study is concerned it refers to all oral and written texts in the language that are recognized and experienced as literature in the community, predominantly for their creative use of the language, fictionality and imaginative qualities[1]. (Negash 77)

Missionaries and Early Translations

Missionaries David Livingstone (1813-1873) and Robert Moffat (1795-883) are reported by historians Tlou and Campbell to have settled among the Tswana people.[2] Their mission was to spread the gospel and convert local people to Christianity. In this process, they

---

[1] Negash, Ghirmai. *A history of Tigrinya literature in Eritrea: (the oral and the written 1890-1991)*. Research School of Asian, African, and Amerindian Studies, University of Leiden, 1999.

[2] Tlou, Thomas, and Alec C Campbell. *History of Botswana*. Macmillan Botswana, 1984.

used translation as a very important mechanism in the service of conversion. For example, this period saw the emergence of the translation of the Gospel of Luke into Setswana, among the first translations performed in the history of Setswana language. Other translations that followed continued in the same trend of seeking to advance the interests of the new Christian religion that undermined important elements of orality in Setswana language. In this regard, Berman, makes the following emphatic point showing that translation was initially and exceptionally associated with the dissemination and consolidation of the Christian faith among Batswana:

Radical changes began after a missionary visitor suggested that Moffat must replace the Dutch hymns with Setswana ones so that the gospel truths in the Setswana language would be fully implanted in the hearts of the Batswana. Moffat then translated the Dutch hymns into Setswana and he also translated Dr. William Brown's catechism (scripture lessons) of 336 questions and answers, the lord's prayer and other related material. (Berman 112)

Foundations of Criticism

Research demonstrates with concrete evidence that translation is historically known to be a very important aspect of Botswana literature. This is shown by the existence of translations and the scholarly criticisms or commentaries. Shole cites Prochazka's assertion that perhaps all literatures of our cultural area start with translations in a way that reiterates the significant role translation has played in the history of Setswana literature (Shole 53). At this point, an attempt to answer some basic but important questions is crucial. The first question to consider is how and when did the work of translation start in Botswana. Furthermore, addressing the question of who the main translators were at a particular point and appreciating who the main translators were needed to be emphasized. Developing an understanding of what debates emanate from the various kinds of translations in Setswana language is also paramount. Finally, as a way of laying the foundation to this work, it is important to use an approach that addresses the origins and development of translation in Botswana by paying close attention to some texts that have been translated from either Setswana or English.

Some Important Questions

In order to successfully develop an argument that places translation in the context of Setswana literature through reviewing published criticisms and translations, the following research questions are presented to help conceptualize and contextualize the criticality of the subject in question: who were the main translators of Setswana literature at a given time in history?; What type of translations did they perform and what were the motivations? What methods or approaches did the translators use? Did the translators write introductions to their works? What is translation in the context of Setswana literature? Who were the main critics of the translated works and what statements did they make about the translated works? What role has translation played in the development of Setswana literature?

III

The theoretical premise of this discussion advocates for a culturally responsive translation approach when translating works of literature. Due to linguistic, cultural and social differences, it is important for translators, more especially creative translators to avoid the use of expressions that are out of context with respect to the culture of a target language. In this specific case, the translation from English into Setswana or vice versa has to use approaches that are relevant by representing some cultural ideas in an unbiased way. In The Translation Studies Reader, Lawrence Venuti offers some key concepts that can generally guide any work of literary translation such as the one under consideration. Venuti theorizes that the exercise of translation can exist both as process and a product. Furthermore, Venuti postulates that "translation dates back to the antiquity or the ancient past especially the period before the middle ages." This particular statement is further developed by the author by focusing primarily on approaches that have been developed in the twentieth century, focusing particularly on the past forty years. To validate his point further, Venuti notes that "it was during this period that translation studies emerged as a new academic field, at once international and disciplinary" (1).

By citing the postulation of a French translator and translation theorist Antoine Berman that "a translator without historical consciousness is a crippled translator, a prisoner of his representation of translation and of those carried by social discourses at the moment," Venuti emphasizes the importance of the work of translation to be more than just changing a document from a source text to a target language" (Venuti 2). As Venuti argues, "scholars of translation as well as translators can significantly advance their work by taking into account the historical contexts in which translation has been studied and practiced" (2).

With respect to individuals who participate in the translation process, Venuti puts emphasis on the need to identify the distinction between a translator and a translation scholar. This is important because the latter engages in different interdisciplinary tasks which are guided by distinct theories of translation. What makes matters more complex, at least as Venuti claims, "is a shared interest in a topic; however, there is no guarantee that what is acceptable as a theory in one discipline or approach will satisfy the conceptual requirements of a theory in others" (Venuti 2). Another important idea that comes from Venuti is relative autonomy as a concept of translation. Technically, this term refers to "factors that distinguish it from the source text and from the texts initially written in the target language. These factors include textual features and strategies performed by the agents who produce the translation, not only the translator but the editors as well" (5). The author submits that the history of translation theory can in fact be imagined as a set of changing relationships between the relative autonomy of the translated text and two other categories, equivalence and function. For Venuti, equivalence is associated with "accuracy," "adequacy," "correctness," "correspondence," "fidelity," and "identity." It is a valuable notion of how the translation is connected to the text (Venuti 5). Function is understood as the potentiality of the translated text to release diverse effects, beginning with the communication of information and ending with the production of a response comparable to the one produced by the source text in its own culture, since translation is also social, function is also the reason why readers are able to respond to the translated work, consequently opening the door for a critical platform (Venuti 5).

Another theorist, Louis Kelly, argues for a 'complete' theory of translation that "has three components: specification of function and goal; description and analysis of operations; and critical comment on relationships between goals and relationships" (1). Similar to Venuti's, Kelly also understands function to mean the potentiality of the translated text to release diverse effects, beginning with the communication of information and the production of a response comparable to the one produced by the source text in its own culture.

Walter Benjamin in his essay titled The Translator's Task speaks about cultural appropriation. Benjamin poses a thought provoking question: "is a translation meant for readers who do not understand the original?" This question is used by the author to develop his argument that "translation is a form and therefore in order to grasp it as such, we have to go to the original" (Benjamin 76). According to Benjamin, "factors that satisfy the translatability of a text are the production of an equivalent literary language in the target text such that the originality of the source language is not only represented in the target text but also transcending it. Put in simple terms what Benjamin views the translated text as a creative work of literature in itself. In fact, according to Benjamin, through translation the original develops into a linguistic sphere that is both higher and purer" (79). For Benjamin, the translator's task is "to find the intention toward the language into which the work is to be translated, on the basis of which an echo of the original is awakened in it" (79-80). This statement emphasizes the fact that every translated text presents a totally unique and new form that presents its own uniqueness.

In *Principles of Correspondence*, Nida discusses the notion of correspondence in translation. He offers a detailed description of different types of translation. Arguing that no two languages are identical, neither in the meanings given to corresponding symbols nor in the ways in which such symbols are arranged in phrases and sentences, it stands to reason that there cannot be absolute correspondence between languages (Nida 141). The author qualifies his statement by citing Rossetti, who asserts that "a translation remains perhaps the most direct form of commentary" (Nida 141). The author also makes mention of the fact that "the translating of some types of poetry by prose may be dictated by important cultural considerations" (142-3). In other words, Nida argues that it is improbable to have a translation that does not reflect the matrix from various elements of culture. Nida, moreover, emphasizes that: "the particular purposes of the translator are also important factors in dictating the type of translation...the primary purpose of the translator may be information as to both content and form. A translator's purposes may involve much more than information" (142-3). This means that different translators generally and normally translate various works for a number of reasons. These include ensuring linguistic and cultural preservation. In the context of Botswana, it can be posited that the intent of the work of translation goes beyond the transmission of information and makes contributions to cultural development ensuring linguistic competence and cultural confidence.

Nida further provides a description of basic orientations in translating. The two main types being formal and dynamic forms of equivalence. The 'formal' is described as that in which the message in the receptor language is matched as closely as possible with the different elements in the source language. Dynamic translation constitutes the relationship between the receptor and message as constitute receptor and message languages as basically the same in their structure and meaning (Nida 144). The importance of drawing the distinction between the two is key for translators to pay attention to if the objective is to produce a communicative text.

In some cases, translators may be faced with challenges that have to do with issues of cultural relevance as they are found in the source language. In this regard, Nida underscores that "when the cultures are related but the languages are quite different, the translator is called upon to make a good many formal shifts in the translation" (Nida 144). The phrase "formal shifts" is important here. It refers to the intuitive ability of the translator to be able to recognize the deeper (hidden) cultural aspects that need to be made relevant through the use of proper equivalents. Nida drives the point home by concluding that, "[however] the cultural similarities in such instances usually provide a series of parallelisms of content that make the translation proportionately much less difficult than when both languages and cultures are disparate. In fact the differences between cultures cause many more severe complications for the translator than do differences in language structure" (Nida 145).

IV

A Brief Historical Survey of Setswana Literature in Translation

Since the focus of this project is specifically on how translation has played a role in developing Setswana literature, a broad historical time frame that dates back to early colonial literature is considered. One of the key arguments held in this work is that translation, having dominated the first written form or orthography of Setswana language, resulted in the development of novel literary traditions in the history of Setswana language. Some of the works that came as a result of this translation are the establishment of newspapers and local journals which were written in both Setswana and English during and after the colonial era. Indeed, as Shole notes, "the earliest forms of modern written literature in Setswana language consisted of translations." In demonstrating this literary historical fact, Shole cites Robert Moffat's Pilgrim's Progress as one of the earliest works under the genre of prose fiction (Shole 53). Robert Moffat was a missionary who had been sent by the London Missionary Society to introduce Christianity in

Southern Africa. After learning the local language, he undertook a number of translation works which included the translation of the bible that aimed at converting the locals to Christianity. Hermanson makes mention of other theological translations carried by missionaries and administrators such as Jan van Riebeeck (6).

After the 18th century, a number of translations were carried by writers in Botswana and South Africa. These were mainly the translation some works by William Shakespeare. Shole highlights that the first dramas in Setswana were translations of William Shakespeare's Comedy of Errors and Julius Caesar. Another interesting development was the translation of Chinua Achebe's Things fall Apart, translated from English into Setswana by D. P. S. Monyaise (Monyaise 1991). At the time, other important translations of the time include Botswana's national anthem which was adapted in 1966, when the country gained independence. Originally written in Setswana, the country's official language, the national anthem has an English translation which is the country's official language.

Translation is a very important and significant tool that was consistently used by missionaries, anthropologists, and possibly colonial administrators. Furthermore, exposure to mainstream Western literature such as the works of Shakespeare and others largely influenced the method of translation that was used at the time. There is evidence that translators, in addition to using a 'word-for-word' approach, also copied the style and the structure such that the end result in Setswana was almost the same as in the English version from which it was translated. Due to this, some important aspects of cultural relevance and contextual meanings were compromised. This confirms the importance of Nida's warning about the inherent risks in every work of translation.

Different methods were used by various translators depending on the time and context of translation: 1) Some used the word-for-word method; 2) Some used the method of equivalence, focusing on meaning rather than words; 3) and a few others also included introductions to their translated texts, with attempt to explain motives and approaches behind each work of translation. Examples of translators who used the word-to-word method are Plaatjie, Raditladi and Seboni; translators who experimented with the method of equivalence include Monyaise, and Schapera. The latter two Monyaise in Dilo di Masoke and Schapera in Praise Poems of the Tswana Chiefs also wrote extended critical introductions to their translations, explicating their methodology.

Major Translations and Translators

The main translators considered in this research project include Raditladi, Monyaise, Plaatje and Schapera. The translation critic, Shole J. Shole who has been a fundamental figure in Setswana translation studies is also considered. Shole's work as a critic is focused on describing aspects of translation and mistranslation to the extent represented in Raditladi and Plaatje's successes and failures to accurately record the cultural translations in Shakespearean plays. His critical study also offers alternatives by providing solutions to errors he sees in the translated Shakespearean plays from English into Setswana. Others who succeeded Raditladi and Plaatje in undertaking literary translations include Seboni and Thedi whose works are also discussed in this study. Together, the works of these translators (Raditladi, Plaatjie, Seboni, and Thedi) and the critical work of Shole constitutes the bulk of the work of Botswana literary productions in translation.

Shole's critical work is important for various reasons. In his critique, he outlines specific aspects of mistranslation or translation problems. Furthermore, he defines and discusses translation works in the context of cultural relevance and faithfulness within the Setswana language. His approach offers an expansive method of looking at translation as an activity that is connected with cultures of both the source and target languages. Shole's main argument is that literary translation should be approached much more carefully since it entails not only linguistic structures but more importantly cultural ones which, in Setswana, is constituted by proverbs, folktales, idioms and other elements of oral literature. According to him, cultural context is crucial because, if not carefully attended to, it can distort the meaning of the original text and the intent of the writer (Shole 52). In this regard, and viewed globally, Shole's view of translation therefore aligns with translation theorists such as Venuti and Kelly.

As for the translators who undertook the translation of Shakespeare's plays, Shole criticizes them for failing to understand cultural elements that tend to prevail in English culture and on the other hand compromise cultural concepts inherent in Setswana culture. Shole believes that the only way that translators could have avoided such mistranslation is by approaching both the source and the target texts faithfully. He emphasizes that the translation of Setswana texts into English and vice versa should always be comparative in its approach such that the translator's consciousness and techniques enters the essence of the text and is visible in the outcome. He further suggests that comparative approaches of translation between languages are far more best suited in the Setswana context rather than a hierarchical approach that may create the privileging of English culture to Setswana. In short, Shole's observations underline that exposure to the styles and methods of writers from both traditions is necessary in translation, and also that there is a need for translators to evaluate critically whether or not the text to be translated is suitable for translation in Setswana.

Plaatjie is among the first leading translators of the pre-independence period. In his publication of 1916, Sechuana proverbs with literal translations and their European equivalents, Plaatje represents a rather distinct form of translation of oral literatures such as the traditional teachings found in the Tswana culture. One of the methods that Plaatjie adopts in his translation practice is the appropriation of Shakespeare's style into the Setswana vernacular. Through this particular method, Plaatjie seems to affirm Setswana's capacity to be used in creative composition and literature, just as Shakespeare did it for English. Plaatjie also uses an approach that closely copies the European style in other works that he translated from English into Setswana. Viewed from a theoretical perspective, Plaatjie's efforts to emulate the Shakespearean style in Setswana can lead to two interpretations. One interpretation can lead to the claim that he deliberately did so in order to show or demonstrate the capacity and vitality of Setswana language in ways that are on par with English. A less sympathetic interpretation is to view his method as a sign of his own cultural assimilation to the European tradition.

Barolong Seboni's work Setswana riddles: translated into English follows the approach that was used by Plaatjie. His translation of Setswana riddles into English indicate not only the belief that Setswana can be translated into English but also that it is possible to translate oral forms to printed ones. However, Seboni's translation technique also differs from Plaatjie's in certain ways. Unlike Plaatjie, who sought equivalents for expression in the source and target languages, Seboni's translation tend to be more literal. Also unlike Plaatjie, Seboni used extensive notes to explain cultural context and meanings behind the expressions.

Semakaleng Monyaise, the translator of Chinua Achebe's Things Fall Apart, attempted to fully capture the original intent of the writer Achebe by retaining its original form. Achebe's orality and storytelling technique are fully retained in the Setswana text by Monyaise. Another translator, Barulaganye Thedi, also used a similar approach to that of Monyaise when translating Bessie Head's When Rain Clouds Gather from English into Setswana. It must be noted however that the works of Thedi and Monyaise are neither preceded nor prefaced in a way that expresses the methodology and underlying theories of their translations.

An In-depth Look into Methods of translation

Fundamentally, one important aspect with regard to trends of translation in the literary history of Setswana literature is to address a question of what translators and translation critics have said in the prefaces and introductions of their works.

In his critical review of both Plaatjie and Raditladi's translations, Shole points out that "these dramas represent three major types of translations, namely literal translation, free translation as well as adaptation. They also illustrate the major achievements and shortcomings of this literary practice in Setswana" (Shole 51). During the translation of the Shakespearean plays, translators adopted two methods that varied in the sense that one entailed making some modifications to the original work but the other did not. Basically, Shole notes that some of the works did not translate well in terms of literary content, but that the translators utilized the same style and theme by using a different language. In addition, Shole states that "in terms of translation studies in Setswana literature, not much attention has been given to literary translations in Setswana, either as translations or works of art on their own, despite the role they have played. Shole posits that even among our reading sector, which consists mainly of students, these translations suffer neglect" (Shole 51). He furthers his statement by comparing the complexity of translating poetry as opposed to other works of literature such as drama. He mentions that "the translation of poetry presents great problems. If the two languages belong to distinct cultures this becomes worse. Images, puns and allusions may become ineffective or fail to make sense" (Shole 57).

In his work, which is thought to succeed the major translation conducted by Plaatjie, Seboni reiterates that the purpose of his translation produced is "to provide a storehouse or treasure trove of Setswana riddles in English for those who want to understand and appreciate the oral traditions and wisdom of Batswana" (Seboni 2011: Intro.). Seboni makes a powerful statement that translation of traditional literature needs to be considered as it is a crucial tool that can be used to record Setswana wisdom. He further notes that "this is a preservation exercise in that the riddles have not only been transformed from the oral into the written, but have also been captured and stored in a second language, one that rules the waves of world literature, the airwaves of communication and the microwaves of technology" (Seboni 2011:Intro.). Seboni's assertion helps to solidify an answer to the question of language that has been asked by critics in the domain of African literature. He explains:

in the translation of the Setswana riddles into English, I have tried to be as literal as possible so that the nuances and idiosyncrasies of Setswana language come out as much as possible. I have also tried to preserve the sentence structure and word order of Setswana as much as was feasible without making nonsense of the meaning in English. In other words, I strive to capture the original Setswana riddle rather than just the equivalent in English (Seboni 2011: Intro.).

However, Seboni at the same time admits that his approach calls for a delicate balance and there are some challenges along the way: "some words, expressions and phrases that are literally not translatable and it is to this extent that I may not have achieved my goal" (Seboni 2011: Intro.).

Seboni's observations about translatability are shared by Schapera. Thinking particularly about the difficulties involved in translating poetry, Schapera notes that "it is not only the European translator who finds such words and phrases unusually difficult, modern Tswana are sometimes puzzled by them [...]. One feature of the vocabulary needs special mention, not because it presents new difficulties to the translator, but because it enables the poet to indulge in what Fowler terms 'elegant variation'. It consists of referring to a single person by several different kinds of name" (Schapera 1965:22). When it comes to translating Setswana poetry, Schapera acknowledges that there are some stylistic and ambiguity challenges that are unique and popular to Setswana tradition but not English. Schapera's observation complements the thoughts presented earlier by Shole, who pointed out the importance of being conversant with the cultures of both the source and target language.

Critics on the Translation of Setswana Bible

Bible translation in Southern Africa was initially conceptualized and executed by either missionary societies or bible societies (Makutoane and Naude 79). For example, "the first translation was published by the Paris Evangelical Society in 1909. This translation is well known and is still in use as the "old translation. The second translation is the Southern Sotho translation, published in 1989 by the Bible Society of South Africa" (Makutoane and Naude 79). This fact demonstrates that the timeframe that define the origins of translation of texts in Botswana date back to the colonial period. This period is marked by the arrival of missionaries such as Robert Moffat and David Livingstone. However, it may be said that the missionaries primarily focused on translating religious literatures such as the bible. The translation of the Bible by missionaries suggests that the focus was mainly on converting locals to Christianity. It can be maintained that this translation of the biblical literature clearly demonstrates the role that translation played in ensuring religious assimilation imposed on Batswana by the colonialists. For example, there are a number of novels (not in translation though) whose plots show immense relationship between events that are recorded in the Bible. In the years that followed thereafter, along with the works of Shakespeare that were translated into Setswana, translation continued, thereby strengthening the argument that Setswana literature has seen a number of translation routes that emanate from the colonial period through to the postcolonial epoch.

Motivations and Method

There were various forms of translations that had been undertaken and these include those that were religion-oriented and those that were of literary or creative nature. Consequently, it is possible to classify such translations according to their original intent such as whether it was for research or religious purposes. As a matter of fact, the Bible, hitherto classified as a religious text, is among the first textual items to be translated and it was to be followed by other literary works. Many of the translations that followed, such as the national anthem, were meant to indicate the extent of patriotism that was later to be followed by the declaration of independence. In terms of its origins, the assertion that translation of texts in Botswana is defined in terms of historical avenues still holds. This is mainly due to the fact that it keeps on changing in terms of focus at any given time. More specifically, focus on literary works that have been translated into either Setswana or English come as an immense contribution to areas of African and comparative literature as well as translation studies.

V

In view of all the work that has been done on translation in terms of how it relates to the development of Setswana literature as a whole, it is plausible that there is wealth in the interesting conclusions that have been drawn by both translators and critics. Translation in the context of Botswana literature has without doubt its origins in the colonial period. Hence, in this part of the project, translated works are discussed critically in terms of how they are mapped into the field of translation and Setswana literary studies. It has been demonstrated that the motives behind the earlier works of translation were based on the urgency of the colonial missionaries to convert the natives to Christianity. Hence, the traditions of translation date back to the colonial period. For example, the earlier works that have been reviewed showed that they were products of colonial literature. In the process, for the first time oral literature of Setswana cultural lore was presented in the written orthography which followed the same alphabet used in the language of the colonizer, or British English in Botswana's context.

It had not always been the case that all the translations of literary genres have been only represented textually because historical evidence has shown that some resulted from transcriptions and some genres were represented in other forms. For example, some folktales were represented as picture illustrations in addition to the written form. However, much work still remains to be researched in this particular area. It is also important to highlight that while appreciating the methods, motives, and some approaches used at the time of translation, many works had been purposefully translated for specific functions. For example, translations were done for educational purposes. It was one of the only, if not the only effective way that the colonialists could depend on in order to be progressive in their undertaking. For example, the earlier discussion on 'The Bible and Translation' clarifies the argument on the functionality of colonial translations for they primarily conferred religious or spiritual education. In this regard, the following paragraphs expound on each specific genre of Setswana literature that is historically known to have been significantly affected by the translation process.

Oral Narratives: Setswana Proverbs and Folktales

Culturally, oral narratives in Botswana were passed down from one generation to another through the process of socialization. However, as a result of translation, there was a number of interesting observations which can allow literary critics to do a comparative study of various forms of literatures of Setswana nature. For example, some proverbs were transcribed into written Setswana and then later translated into English. In addition to avoiding literal translation, a noticeable attempt to use the equivalents in target languages is also noted. However, while this has been problematic and dismissed by critics such as Shole as lacking the relevant, authentic and aesthetic cultural appeal, this method has been very effective in internationalizing the content of Setswana literature. In this regard and on the basis of several comparisons, it has been possible to draw some similarities and comparisons between Setswana and English translations.

Setswana folktales stand out when compared with translated proverbs because they went through a threefold process of translation. Firstly, the folktales transitioned from the oral to the written, then secondly they were translated into English. The third aspect, which is hitherto recommended for another study is that many folktales also existed in the form of pictures. It has also been availed for teaching at primary schools. This method is, arguably, one of the most important translation developments that can also be used to speculate on the role that translation has played in building Setswana literature for children. Many other folktales from various parts of Africa have also gone through the same process, and because of this they can be studied comparatively. This is viewed in this work as one interesting hallmark of translation which can be studied critically, in the same way as other translated works have been studied.

Through the work of translators such as Plaatjie and Seboni, it has been shown that some of the proverbs in Setswana language were translated into English. In some instances, where the process of translation became a challenge, an attempt to look for equivalents in the target language by the translators was made. While proverbs, just like folktales have oral traditions, it is important to draw conclusions that it is through the process of translation that they were first converted to the written forms by way of transcribing them and then they were later translated into other languages. In this case, such proverbs can be said to have sustained a twofold process which entailed having to be put first in the written Setswana orthography and then later translated into English. Another significant aspect to take into consideration about such proverbs is that while in the precolonial period they were passed from one generation to another, through the process of translation it was possible for them to exist in written forms and be preserved.

Poetry: The Oral and the Written

Oral poems in Setswana have been first transcribed and then translated into English. Schapera's method which was discussed earlier has been the basis of the criticism that follows. The translations of Schapera were primarily influenced by anthropological research which sought to explain cultures of Setswana speaking societies to the colonial scholarship. Thus his use of the translated term 'praise poetry' does not fully represent 'poko' as perceived by the people themselves. Schapera's translation, therefore, focuses on only one aspect of 'praise' and this problematic approach excludes other features of these poems such as criticizing, ridiculing, indigenous humor, mockery and insult which we cannot say they are praising in nature. His translation, and many other works by other researchers that used the term 'praise poetry' only focus on a single aspect and may result in some misconceptions on what this type of poetry does according to the Tswana customs. In addition, the translations of the poems are not 'culturally complete' as according to the customs of the Tswana. They are culturally accompanied by ululation and choruses. In that sense, it can be said that the textual representation of these translations omit the orality and therefore do not fully represent the complete forms.

Prose: Novels and Plays

As shown in section IV, a few novels and plays from English have been translated into Setswana. An outstanding example in this category is the translation of Chinua Achebe's Things fall Apart into Setswana by Monyaise. Plays that were translated imitated the style and the form of Shakespearean plays. Two examples in this style are: Plaatje's *Diphosophoso* and Raditladi's *Dintshontsho tsa Lorato*. Interestingly, the translation of Shakespearean plays into Setswana influenced the nature of plays that followed thereafter to a very large extent. This contributed to the development of Setswana literature in general, having a significant effect on the structure of Setswana novels and plays that followed thereafter, including those that were not written in English or those that never went through the translation process.

Biblical Literature and Colonialism

Critics such as Lamin O. Sanneh (1990) emphasized the "centrality of translation to the Christian religion". Sanneth further notes that, "when we take translation seriously, we find that the rules according to which the enterprise succeeds or fails are generally determined by indigenous paradigms" (95). There are some consequences associated with this and they may be used to support the contention that a critical study of translation in indigenous literatures should be overemphasized. The translation of the bible into Setswana language can thus be analyzed by placing it in various postcolonial contexts. For example, an observation that "readers of the Southern Sotho translations are held prisoner by Western translators by denying them the right to biblical texts received and interpreted on their own terms as religious artefacts from the ancient Mediterranean world" cannot be doubted (Makutoane and Naude 80).

Conclusions and Recommendations

In the Setswana Society, translation has historically played an important role. It was used by missionaries, anthropologists, and possibly colonial administrators to advance some colonial interests. Translation has also been used as a tool by colonizers to assimilate to the English language as well as influence literary forms of Setswana literature. Furthermore, exposure to mainstream Western literature, such as the works of Shakespeare and others, largely influenced the methods used in translation. There is evidence that local translators in addition to using 'word-for-word' approach, copied the style and the structure such that the result was almost the same except for the language that was used. In that process, some important aspects such as cultural relevance and contextual underpinnings were compromised. In addition to the translations produced by some European missionaries and anthropologists, some natives of Setswana who had received a Western education also participated in the art of translation. There were scholarly commentaries and criticism that responded to the works that had been translated. Some translations included 'introductions' that sought to explain motives and approaches behind each work of translation. Some genres such as proverbs and folktales were not only translated in form and structure, that is from oral to written orthography, but they were translated into a different language. For example, some of the works were first translated into Setswana and later translated into English. Much can be said about the aesthetic detachment influenced by this occurrence. For example, folktales were oral and could not take any other form, at least according to the custom of being narrated at night, but now they were available in writing and in record. They were not passed on from one generation to another by word of mouth as was the custom of the Batswana. The translation of texts has led to literary criticism which can be applied to the postcolonial discourses that relate to Setswana literature. This area of study includes the important different literary genres of Setswana nature that continue to be studied critically as a systematic whole as well as in relation to the African-language literatures.

Keith Phetlhe
Ohio University,
College of Fine Arts,
School of Interdisciplinary Arts
Athens. Ohio. USA

References

Berman, Sidney K. "Analysing the Frames of a Bible: The Case of the Setswana Translations of the Book of Ruth." University of Bamberg Press, 2014.

Berman, Sidney K. "Cognition and context in translation analysis: contextual frames of reference in Bible translation." *Scriptura* 113.1 (2014): 1-12.

Hermanson, Eric A. "A brief overview of Bible translation in South Africa." *Acta Theologica* 22.1 (2004): 6-18.

Johnson, David. "Shakespeare and South Africa." Oxford, Clarendon Press, 1996.

Makutoane, TJ, and JA Naude. "Colonial interference in the translations of the Bible into Southern Sotho." *Acta Theologica Supplementum* 12 (2009): 79-94.

Monyaise, Semakaleng D.P. "Dilo di Masoke." Chinua Achebe. Heinemann Southern Africa, 1991.

Negash, Ghirmai. *A history of tigrinya literature in Eritrea: The oral and the written, 1890-1991.* Research School of Asian, African and Amerindian Studies (CNWS), Universiteit Leiden, 1999.

Okpewho, Isidore. "African Oral Literature." Bloomington: Indiana UP (1992).

Plaatje, Solomon Tshekisho. "Sechuana proverbs with literal translations and their European equivalents." K. Paul, Trench, Trubner & Company, 1916.

Raditladi, Leetile D. "Dintšhontšho tsa loratô." Bona Press, 1965.

Raditladi, Leetile Disang. "Motšwasele II." Witwatersrand University Press, 1970.

Sanneh, Lamin. "'They Stooped to Conquer': Vernacular Translation and the Socio-Cultural Factor." *Research in African Literatures* 23.1 (1992): 95-106.

Schapera, Isaac. "Praise-poems of Tswana chiefs." Isaac Schapera. Oxford University Press, 1965.

Seboni, Barolong. "Setswana riddles: translated into English." Petlo Literary Arts Trust, 2011.

Seddon, Deborah. "Shakespeare's Orality: Solomon Plaatje's Setswana Translations." *English Studies in Africa* 47.2 (2004): 77-95.

Shakespeare, William, and Solomon T Plaatje. "Diphosophoso: E fetoletswe mo puong ya Setswana." Botswana Book Centre, 1974.

Shole, Shole J. "Shakespeare in Setswana: An Evaluation of Raditladi's Macbeth and Plaatje's Diphosophoso." *Shakespeare in Southern Africa* 4 (1990): 51-64.

Shole, Shole J. "An evaluation of some drama translations in Setswana." *South African Journal of African Languages* 3.1 (1983): 1-38.

Thedi, Barulaganye. *Fa Maru a Kokoana.* Bessie Head. Heinemann Boleswa, 1991.

Chapter 1

Immediately after the entire congregation bowed, the church leader, Moagi Ramarepetla, never waited to be asked to lead the church in prayer. He called upon the almighty, the God of Christians. His voice roared just like that of thunder in the clouds, until its effect was more or less like that of the buzzing noise made by a bee flying inside the water calabash. His voice roared and deepened until it shook the sand that those who had come to worship had bowed down on. It was evident that he was possessed by some form of a spirit. It was unlikely that his voice came from such a tiny chest, but putting that aside, like red hot metal burning a piece of cloth his voice touched the hearts of believers and nonbelievers. It was certain that he was being controlled by a force that was clearly not of this earth.

Chilly wind in the morning stopped the turbulence, as if wanting to pay attention to the church leader as he spoke with the creator. The banks of Metsimotlhabe river looked as if they were amazed by this occurrence as well. No object seemed to be moving nor shaking. A lot of trees whose leaves had fallen because it was July stood still awaiting the spring to arrive.

As Modiko was listening to the prayer, he remembered that it was said that such big streams like Sekokomogo were a habitat for very big dragons called dikgwanyape. That was the reason why the stream was always flowing with water. He was told by his paternal aunt that the waters of Kolobeng river could even fill up during winter when the rains would have long gone, but the dragon inside this river was capable of drinking up all this water. At night, when people are asleep, this dragon would fly to Tshwaanyane pond in Molepolole where it would fill up its belly with this water. It is reported that the eyes of this kgwanyape light up during the night and anyone who sees this light dies instantly. Modiko was very frightened that this dragon would swallow him up when he got baptized. Alas, it would be better to be swallowed by the dragon than to have one's eyes blast in the fire of the devil. Ija! Imagine those scorpions and centipedes and millipedes as big as elephants...

When Modiko's thoughts came back from daydreaming, he reckoned that the church leader was now calling to God as if they were talking face to face, with rigid eye contact. The voice of the church leader was similar to that of a baby after crying for a very long time but now almost to the point of appreciating comfort. That is why when he closed his prayer, he said:

> "We will not pray to you for very long time or yell at you as if calling Ba'al, the idol god, or as if we are calling out to a God that is very far when we are calling to you, the God that is quick to hear. We are calling unto you the shield of all nations, the shield, the blanket that protects the nations. Oh! the white cow that is chosen, the good one who desires us to live. 'It is to the eagle that has something to offer that we raise our heads to, but a person with empty hands, we push his family aside.' We will not be long in our plea, as if we are eating the skull of an ass, when we are calling unto YOU who knows what brings us here. That's why we are here to baptize your children so that you may accept them at the end of this system of things. Let them be the flock that fear you, with loyalty, one that will be saved when the wicked are destroyed. We are asking for all this in the name of Jesus Christ our Lord and Saviour."

At once and in oneness, the congregation responded in a loud voice and said: "Amen! Haleluya!" The congregation erupted with a hymn that talked about a beautiful river where people could wash away their sins. Pastor Ramarepetla wiped off his sweat with a dirty piece of cloth, and then joined the congregation in singing as he wiped away the soil from his knees.

The service and baptism were assigned to be done by Evangel Jeremiah Letlotla, who was known by the believers and the wicked to have a very soft voice, like that of a woman in conversation, but when he was preaching the word of God, he could roar like a lion. When praying, his voice would paralyze and consume the audience just like the snake that catches a rodent with the delicacy of its eyes. His small eyes were enveloped inwardly by his eye pockets and they kept on emitting some star-like flashes. His face was flat with the tiny eyes that were so close to each other such that they didn't match such a wide face. The nose was very tiny, like that of a chick's dropping. It is only his ears that made a perfect match to that giant head since they were like the leaves of the mhawa tree. His neck was very fat so that it could carry the head of a buffalo. His body was that of a giant, with considerable height, strength and very puffy like that of someone who used to be a boxer when he was still a boy.

When he took the slate that Moses once threw down in frustration, Jesus' book, one that it is believed that people read it widely but interpret it differently until they end up walking in confusion; he saw the July sun showing up where the earth intersects with the sky. The women kept on squeezing the blankets underneath their feet so as to protect themselves against the cold sand. Young women and men were shrunken as the chill air kept them company. Ramarepetla was the only one wiping off sweat. His small limbs, which appeared as if they had grown from his belly, had a hard time trying to wipe away the sweat around his waist as it ran profusely from his reddish hair down to his neck. Evangel Letlotla glanced at the congregation and then announced where the reading of the word was from. He took his spectacles and then placed them to his eyes; then he started reading from the bible. He read slowly with eloquence and very carefully like that of a person who had great respect for the work that he was doing. After he finished reading, he took off the spectacles and placed them in the pouch. He then replaced them with sunglasses, ones that did not allow the congregation to see his eyes. He did not use the voice of a baby like he did before, his voice deepened until it was like that of a bull, but not like that of the devil.

"The congregation of the living God," he took off his dark sunglasses and his small eyes produced some first rain lightening-like emissions as he looked at the congregation. He then continued:

"I would like to specifically address the baptismal candidates. Getting baptized is no joke. I just read to you how John baptized our

3

Lord. After that the Lord went ahead and resisted the enemy- The Devil. Why? The Lord was now a newly born creature. He had left the flesh and its desires at the fountain. Some of you here are witches, adulterers, gossipers, slanderers, etcetera. But seeing that you came to this river, we have hope that you want to leave behind such bad ways because, at last, they bring death and unquenchable fire, one that does not cease to burn like that of borankana[1] fueled with the sheep's fat."

Modiko felt as if the words were directed to him, and just like moga thorns the words struck him. He remembered a red-hot glowing coal that once got into Modise's shoe. He remembered how Modise yelled like a small baby though he was a grown man, with his beard almost covering his face. He screamed at the top of his lungs like an old female pig. He roared in pain as the hot coal burnt his flesh and the shoe, he kept closing and opening his eyes and laid his head on the ground, but all this while he would never close his mouth. He yelled like a hen trapped on her eggs. He did not allow anyone to come close to him, but after some time he quenched his leg in a bucket full of water. But now, when Modiko thought of how sinners would be covered with hellfire, he could not wait for that to happen to him.

After such a scary sermon, Evangel Letlotla, Modiko's father, instructed all the baptismal candidates to line up. One of the young men in the congregation had already brought a long stave which he used to measure the depth of Sekokomoge river. This young man then gave the stave to Evangel Letlotla, who then got into the water until he was satisfied with the depth. The first baptismal candidate came with the support of two young men who gave her to the evangelist. The poor skinny woman was already shaking, and evangel Letlotla held her delicately and asked for her name.

"My name is Ntshipi, Sir," the woman responded.

"What is your surname?"

"Ntshipi Motlogelwa."

---

[1] Traditional dance of Setswana culture

The two were looking at each other such that the evangelist put his hands on the woman's shoulders. He then said a short prayer which he finished by saying: "In the name of the Father, the Son and the Holy Spirit, I baptize Ntshipi Motlogelwa to be your disciple."

By saying that, he submerged the woman in the water. The water covered her head and the body and the evangelist held her under the water for quite some time, he took her out when she started shaking. With her mouth wide open, the women wiped off the water using her hand as she came out of the water. She then started coughing like a choked goat, her thin legs were quaking. It was almost sunset when the baptism was completed. The congregation was led by evangelists with those who were getting baptized in the middle. Everyone was leaving the river side to the place where the candidates were to be given instructions and welcomed as newly found members of Motlha-o-Etla Church. The herdboys who had come to witness this fascinating activity of elderly people swimming in the river went back to their fathers' cattle as they conversed about what they saw. They were amazed by the fact that the kgwanyape, which is said to be in the river, did not eat these people from the church.

****

When one is at the top of Moruakgomo hill and then looks at the terrain of the village of Molepolole, the village is scattered in the open area like the herd of cattle grazing in the yawning land of the Kgalagadi. But because the village is built in an area that is separated by small streams, the traditional Setswana houses and rondavels, the appearance of the houses is very patchy and dark, just like dried cow dung, but they continue like that until they are stopped by the stream. In the winter, the rivers are covered with dried brownish grass. On the hilly terrains of Tsoditsokwane, one is likely to find the accumulating red dust at first sight. The winds, which are said to possess the power from the metallic millipede with the noisy, rattling metals, and has the thing that is having water and fire in the same mouth at the same time,

5

catches anyone who comes down its metal road.[2] They provoke the red dust which ends up filling the rest of the village.

****

Upon looking to the east, the village lies rapt like a pumpkin until the view is blurred. The rondavel houses are squeezed in and arranged into the clans. The walls are colorfully decorated using different soils. The corrugated iron rooftops shine in the winter sun that hides in the clouds and would count up to two or three. At the far back of the yard, there would be another house. This house that is built at the back, it is the women only who know its function. The village is quite lengthy towards the east and the houses get smaller and smaller. The village is surrounded by hills from the south. These hills lie in the open area like an old man's jacket left in the scorching sun to kill the ticks in it. The area at the top of the hill is very flat so that the cattle may graze freely as if they are on the ground. At the south east of the hill lies Kobokwe's cave which is the ancestral home of Bakwena. It is said that Mmadipela, a very big snake that is as long as these hills, stays here.[3]

The Tshwaanyaane river passes through these hills just like a black mamba that sways through the bushy grass. Towards the south of the hills where the Tshwaanyane river starts, to the eastern side of Kobokwe's cave, the Whiteman, said to have brought protection to Botswana, erected a very huge wall with the hope of stopping the water from flowing. What a lie!

This is the kind of lie that can cause one to be struck by lightning even in a cloudless sky with no evidence of possible rain! The water covers up part of the wall with sand that piles up until it reaches the wall's top. On the other side of the wall, the water has dug a very large gully where it flows, leaving a pretty small stream. Towards the east, there are some rocks that appear at the surface of the water. They are

---

[2] Train

[3] Mmadipela is the name of a snake, however *Pela* refers to a rockrabbit. I thought it fit not to translate the name of the snake so that the original meaning is retained.

very tall, as if they could touch the sky. There is a very large mhawa tree which lies in the water; its leaves also lie on the surface of the stream. It is told that mmadipela drinks up all the water in the stream during the night after she comes out of these huge leaves.

"While my husband was still alive," this is what an old woman, Ramakudula's father said of this mhawa tree; "one of the sheep from the flock he was shepherding went astray and climbed up the mhawa tree. When he tried to stop it by climbing up the tree, he saw a very big eye!" The old woman lifted up the cup and faced to the direction of her audience. "A very, very, very big eye! This cave of Kobokwe goes underneath the rocks from mhawa trees by the stream." That's how the old women finished her storytelling. Those who were listening were quite anxious to hear about the end of her story. This was mainly because there is a belief that people who get to see such gigantic snakes tend to wet their pants even if it isn't raining. The man who sees that creature makes his way home crawling like a baby after having lost his mind.

The Dikoloi clan is located near Moruakgomo hill which sits at a distance from the gullies of Dinti. An old man by the name of Tlholego was smoking his pipe, suckling it like a baby breastfeeding from its mother. He released a heavy cloud of bluish smoke to the air. There is a story that one day, as he was sitting under the mogonono tree and smoking his pipe at his yard in Lesilakgokong, everyone ran for their lives when a big blank mamba fell from the tree. At once, Rre Tlholego jumped and struck the snake dead with a rod. Although the snake tried to move, it was dead after its second attempt. By the time he used his rod to strike it once again the snake was already cold. From that day on, his children and wife trusted their father's pipe.

Rre Tlholego sat with other men at his home at the clan of Dikoloing. All the men were passing some time together around the late afternoon while sipping some traditional beer that was prepared by Rre Tlholego's wife Mogatsabanna. At this home, there were four houses. The big one was at the front of the yard and that was the one where Rre Tlholego and his wife slept. The other two houses at the back of the main house were next to and facing each other. Located at the far back of the yard is another house which is used as a sesigo or a keep and many other things that may not be mentioned. The house was full of grain because it was winter just after a great harvest. There were plenty of sorghum bags packed on top of each other in the house. At the back of these sorghum bags lay the sesigo. There is a story that whenever Rre Tlholego was invited to drink traditional beer with other men, he used to go and check the sorghum bags in the house and then he would pat his chest with pride and say: "My sorghum, I know very well that I am not the one who is being invited but you. Everyone here knows that tomorrow they could happen to pass by my place and benefit by being served some of my wheat." After he would say that, he walked with pride to wherever he was invited. As the beer calabash kept going down, Rre Tlholego called his wife to fill it up. She hurriedly came with the beer and poured it slowly in the calabash until it formed some white foam. After that, Mogatsabanna went back to run her chore of preparing the beer. Her husband noticed a scar on her face and remembered how he once hit her using a thick mogonono stick which he pulled out from the earth out of anger. He hit her on the head until she lay unconscious. The fight started because of his wife's religion. It happened so many years ago. Mogatsabanna was a member of Motlha-o-Etla church. One day, during the Lord's Day, she left the sorghum in the fields and went to her church hoping that God would keep the doves and sparrows away. Well, apparently God did not hear her prayer. All the doves and birds from Lesilakgokong infested the harvest and ate until nothing was left. By the time she returned from the church she found Rre Tlholego in a very bad shape, burning with fury. He was very agitated and fuming. Upon asking his wife where she was coming from, she told him that she was from the church. He then asked her again to tell him if she was his wife or the church's.

"I'm your wife," she responded in a quiet voice.

"Then if you are my wife I will discipline you. I will show you your mother now." He roared in a loud voice like a he-goat that was getting castrated. As he shouted he pulled the thick stick of mogonono tree and then hit her very hard on the head such that she fell on her behind.

The children ran crying into the nearby bush. Since that day, Mogatsabanna quit the church and became a housewife.

As the men were drinking their beer with Rre Tlholego, each one of them was actually conversing with whoever he was facing. As they continued talking, one of Rre Tlholego's grandchildren came by. The child burst up in tears and mentioned that he was hungry.

"Why don't you cook for yourself?" the woman said. All the men instantly changed the subject and started talking about school. "Children nowadays go to school while they are still very young. You see even this little fellow here goes to school," Rre Tlholego said while looking at his grandchild.

"This is done deliberately so that they only learn one vowel even though they are paying school fees," Rre Modise said while he was stroking the old scar from the burn of a hot coal. "You know what...the white man and teachers have tricks to make money. Long ago, one would go to the cattle post and do the hunting first, after he had grown up, that was when he could be sent to school."

"But the main reason why these kids keep on repeating the same grade at school is because they cannot understand just one English word," Motlhabane said. He came from the Majatsie clan and he was the only one who had gone to school amongst the group of men. He would never refuse to be reminded that he only attended two weeks of the first grade and then left. He looked at the men, peering into each one of them until he could see that they were anticipating hearing his story. He took all the time sniffing from his nose holes so that the dark-black accumulated heap of the snuff showed. Then he said, "there's only one difficult word in the English language and that word is 'êntê'. It is giving the children a very hard time! But this is where the problem is—" he quickly glanced at the men, as if he was checking if they were paying attention, "—this word may mean two things: first, it could mean 'le' such that we can say 'Tlholego and Modise'. Secondly, this word may be used as 'mme' which doesn't necessarily mean 'to give something out' but as in when you want to say, 'Ramolaisi came here then he said something and then left!' Now you see where the difficulty of this word is? It is just because of this one word."

"What…?" One of the men asked with considerable excitement and curiosity.

"That is simply how it is."

The men could have gone on talking about this but they were disturbed by the arrival of the group of men who came from the Maakathata regiment. Upon realizing that the regiment was facing and advancing towards Rre Tlholego's home, all the men, about four of them who were much younger than Rre Tlholego, disappeared into thin air just like rats would do upon seeing a wild cat. Motlhabane ran through the back gate and behind him ran two men as fast as they could with their knees almost touching their chins almost like bullets. Modise quickly hit the door and immediately hid in the sesigo. He piled all the reddish sorghum on him and then used one of the baskets to conceal his face. He then waited there to see what would happen next. Tlholego stood by the wall to see what the regiment was up to.

"Good morning Major Sergeant"! The leader of the regiment greeted Rre Tlholego from a distance.

This man was greeting Rre Tlholego according to the position he held when he went to fight the battle of the Whiteman against Hitler. He then changed the way and came to Rre Tlholego. The men talked for a while and as they conversed, they kept on pointing at the house of Evangel Letlotla. The regiment leader looked very disturbed and he wore a face of someone who had tasted a poorly brewed traditional beer. In agony he said, "Major Sergeant, you know that he that is being sent by the chief cannot refuse. I really wonder why Jeremiah can't quit this church of his. What has your brother's son eaten? The chief has ordered us to go after them in Metsimabe".

"Don't worry- just do according to the chief's command. The chief is always the messenger of the ancestors. I have tried very hard to talk to Letlotla's son about these whiteman's gods and church that he is following but he doesn't listen. It is said that if a man swallows a morula nut, he trusts the widening of his buttocks."

The regime leader joined other men who were about to go up the hill. The men disappeared from sight as they advanced towards Metsimabe. Rre Tlholego watched them carefully until the last of them disappeared in the maologa trees. He then went to the sesowa and then shouted, "Hey Modise, come out! Those men are chasing after the insane followers of Motlhaoetla. They are not looking for tax like we had thought."

Modise came out of the sesigo and the sorghum grains were dropping from his pockets and shoes. The children who were around covered their mouths because they were very amused. They wanted to laugh at this happening. He angrily gave them an eye like that of a woman whose husband is being taken by another one. The children ran away until they finally broke out in laughter.

Chapter 2

"Please speak up brother, I can't quite hear you. When are they going to come?" The pastor asked.

"I think they will probably be here very soon," Ramarepetla replied.

"Where did you leave them?"

"I left them when they were reaching the road from Mosopa. Evangel Letlotla then asked me to ride here with the bicycle so that I warn you that the men will be here before time. He was hoping that you were in Semarule and instructed that I should call you. I thank God for sending you here. The bicycle gave me some problems along the way. I think they have now passed Thamaga and are on their way to Gametsimabe." Ramarepetla wiped his sweat.

Pastor Keitumetse Mmolaaditso used a well ironed white cloth to wipe away the sweat. His brownish clothes tightened on his huge body, almost similar to that of a woman. The buttons which always sprung off were very tight. The shirt wanted to make way for this huge belly inside it. In his attempt to scratch his belly he stretched his hand as if it was not his. He stretched his limb to the front and then stretched his fingers and then began scratching on the shirt. He saw a very hard time in doing that and went on to wipe the sweat on his ears which were plunged on his fatty head. His ears were as thick as cactus leaves,— thick and fat. His hair was white and short. He liked to comb his hair neatly until it looked like fur. His teeth seemed to be the only problem because they were uneven and scattered like rafters of an old house.

He opened the bible and closely inspected it with a serious face. He hissed like sorghum porridge in a pot as his chest came out slowly. The lips vibrated slowly as he read from the holy book. He read with focus and eventually forgot about what had surrounded him.

****

The Maakathata regiment was approaching from the road near the eastern side of the valley and the men were talking about many things. At first they talked about the insane people like followers of Motlha-o-Etla and about other 'artificial' churches.

"What kind of church would it be without a Whiteman as its pastor?" Moitshopari asked.

"It is said that there are so many roads to finding wealth but there is a few who can follow that path. The main reason why people like Mmolayaditso are so fat is because they are enjoying church contributions. Where on earth have you seen such an old man always swimming with children with the claim that he is baptizing them?" Montsho said. The other men laughed abruptly and then continued talking.

"I swear I would send off my wife back to her mother if she could do such things. What kind of churches take place at night?"

"It is faith my brother. Faith is like grass. No matter how much you like you just can't take it from someone. It is not rooted from facts. A believer cannot confess about their reason to believe on something." Mogami added, he came from Morwa clan. He was the only one who looked afflicted by the assignment they were about to execute. When other men in the regiment laughed at Montsho's joke he and the leader of the regiment were the only ones who didn't laugh. He continued moving amidst the men and making some rattling noise as his shoe frictioned against the gravel. He continued:

"Regardless of how much we can persecute Motlhaoetla followers we can never defeat them. Actually, the more persecution and affliction we bring them, it is as if we are planting the grass after digging it off. Its roots will continue to grow everywhere even where it is not desired. When we make them suffer, Bakwena will sympathize with them in large numbers and eventually join them. Even worse, they will hate us and this chieftaincy. When they are at prison, they will preach to the prisoners and their population will continue to increase. Actually, it is one way of making them multiply and multiply. When you persecute believers, they get strengthened and encouraged in their faith more

14

than before," he ended. Afterwards, he wiped his beard which looked like a wild cat's.

"Let me get this straight Mogapi, or whatever you say your name is Mogami..." Montsho barked like a bulldog.

"I'm Mogami sir," he quietly responded.

"...are you one of them or what? Why are you talking as if you are shielding them? Perhaps you're like a policeman who is being sent to arrest his own mother? Tell us man! Let us know that Tšhibeng-ga-ketswe!"

All the men laughed their teeth out. Some of them fell on their backs and even had their eyes filled with tears from laughter. Those who did not hear the joke asked for it to be shared. A few who stopped laughing managed to share a story of how Mogami got this name.

It was told that one day when men were conscripted to go to a war between the British and the Germans a regiment was sent out to go and search for men in the lands and cattle posts. They were to be taken for military training in Lobatse where they were taught how to use rifles. Mogami was sitting at his lands in Gakgatla enjoying his watermelon and telling boys some stories about how good life was at the mines. After that he told the boys that he would never go to the war which all men were being conscripted into.

"What I've heard is that it is just for the British and the Germans, it is very far from us and we have nothing to do with it. It is said that the German king, Hitler, is fighting the British monarch called Churchill. The fight of these two men was started by Churchill after he married a very beautiful lady, the Queen who is the daughter of King George. Now Hitler wants to use force to take the Mmamosadinyana from Churchill. And Churchill cannot take that nonsense. These men are fighting for this girl. I don't therefore see the point in going to risk our lives fighting for people who are fighting for a girl. We fought the Ndebele of Mzilikazi by ourselves. This is none of our business and the war does not mean anything to us at all. Perhaps Bangwato could go there and risk their lives. We, Bakwena, have got nothing to do with this war...."

"I can see a group of men approaching from the Mmaketlhoetsweng's field," a young lad who had gone to stop a goat from entering the ploughing field warned. His tshega was stuck on his buttocks and it looked pretty much like the tongue of a dog.

"Where are they?" Mogami asked. He had a sizable portion of the watermelon in his mouth. A reddish substance from the watermelon hung loosely on his beard.

It was not necessary for the boy to show him again. He saw around fifty men who held machetes and sticks approaching. They were just by the corner of the ploughing field, just a stone's-throw away. Mogami swiftly ran away like an animal feeling the pain of hot powder put in its eyes. Like a donkey that likes sorghum he pounced and struck open the branches by the gate using his chest. The boys could see him running as fast as could towards the Moumakwa pond. When the regiment arrived, they instantly asked the boys about the whereabouts of their father. A small boy who saw the men from a distance showed them. They could spot him running very fast past a huge mokgalo tree.

They immediately started chasing him. It was a very hectic marathon with a man running his feet to the limit. Mogami swayed through the trees, running as fast as he could. From the fastness of his pace he appeared much smaller, like a baby. Considering his pace and the size he had assumed, one could even think that he could fit very well in a small bucket. He was compacted, squeezed and looking very tiny. He found his brother's wife Mma Ketlhoetsweng very busy cutting and piling up chunks of grass. Mogami then jumped into the grass and squeezed his body beneath. Mma Ketlhoetsweng knew immediately that the dogs of George had started so she never asked anything. She continued piling up the stalks of grass on top of Mogami.

As the men arrived at the woman, they asked her if she had not seen a man in the run. She pointed forward claiming that the man they were talking about had run further yonder. Whereas the younger men continued to chase after him, the elderly men stopped for a while. Each one of them pulled the stalk of grass so as to sit down and rest. They were shocked to realize that a skunk could have rotted in the woman's grass.

"What is smelling so bad, Bakwena?" One of them asked.

"Isn't it a rat that could have probably died in the grass?" Another one remarked in his confusion.

"No way, this does not smell like a rotten rat. I think it is fart." The third one added.

It didn't take a while, the fright Mogami had immediately caused his stomach to grumble. Even a deaf person could have heard the noise made by his grumbling stomach. At once all men jumped and started un-piling the stalks of grass from where he hid. Mogami quickly jumped like a pig that had swallowed a poisonous substance. This time you couldn't see the movement of his legs as he ran. It was evident that before that he was not running but playing. His legs resembled the planks on the wheels of a very fast horse cart. He was amazingly fast. The old men called the other young men who had chased him and they all followed him, but it was too late. All they could see was the footsteps from his marathon.

Mogami found Rapula chopping some branches which he used to make the wall of the goat kraal. He glimpsed at him, not even to say the greetings. He erupted: "You're still here? The chief's dogs are coming down here. Unless you want to die at the battle that you have absolutely nothing to do with—where its owners will hide behind you?"

By so saying he opened the door of a room that had a newly born baby. He then got into the bed, covered his head and smeared letsoku on his face. The mother of the baby had gone to the backside house of the homestead. When Rapula heard this from Mogami he did not waste time. He jumped thrice and hid inside the hole which had been dug on the foundation and then pulled the lid of the beer pot to conceal himself. "Mosele wa pula o etšwa go sale gale," he happily said as he squeezed himself underneath the hole.

When the woman returned, she was astonished to see a bearded man on the same bed with the baby. Before she could say "his feet are probably hot," Mogami put the pointing finger in his lips and cautioned her to keep quiet. The woman then knew that something was wrong. When you see a dog sleeping at the fireplace, then it cannot

17

withstand the cold. The women saw a group of men entering the place. She knew how terrible this was. As Mogami heard the marching of the regiment outside he pinched the baby and it cried like it had been thrown in the fireplace. When the men saw a log of wood placed near the house they knew that it was a taboo for men to get inside the house with a newborn baby. They went to the backyard and realized that there was nowhere a person could hide. Those who remained outside could spot some fresh chopping of wood. They inquired for whoever was doing the chopping. The woman said that it was a boy who had gone to milk the cows. They went on.

After this incident, the story of a man who slept in a house of a newborn because he was a coward became a very common story in the village. When the men came back from the war they were praised because it was believed that they had gone to fight for Botswana. All those men like Mogami, who had run away from going to war were given mocking names such as dipharameseseng, bokgole-ya-tshiba, bokhibeng-ke-tswe who run away from war by wearing a dress. That's why all men could not stop laughing when Montsho called Mogami "Tšhibeng-ga-ke-tswe."

Mogami got very, very agitated. He felt something blocking his throat. He wanted to kill and his heart was beating very fast. Like a small baboon seeking protection from its mother he jumped at once and strangled Montsho. He blocked all the veins pumping blood in Montsho's body until he started feeling the effect. Montsho could feel that he was losing his soul, just like the glow of moitaletsi lamp that can't survive when there is wind. He opened his mouth and roared like a toad that sees a pound that is filled with water. Now he had become a laughing-stock of all the men who were amused by the joke he had passed earlier. They all thought it was a sign of stupidity. The leader of the regiment came running and, like a cattle egret removing a tick from a cow, he plucked Mogami by his neck. After that, he began yelling and threatening the two men that he could tell the chief about their bad manners. Silence pervaded the place as all men marched but it was broken when the men crossed Tshwaanyane. As they advanced, the hills at the back looked green because of the further distance. The voices of the baboons also stopped eventually. The sunset was about to envelope itself by the sand dunes of the Kgalagadi. All the men started pulling out their huge black jackets which the school boys had mockingly named 'Mesonokannyoko'. Some of the jackets were very dirty and breaking on the collars. The southern wind started blowing as the sun sets. It swept all the clouds in the sky but left the glittering of a few stars. The glittering stars were like the eyes of a bunch of shy girls. As darkness enveloped the place the trees looked like humans. The night birds broke off in their cry and further to the Semarule rocks one could hear a jackal roaring. Some fires set at the homesteads could be slightly spotted. During this time, no one would dare to pass near Kobokwe's cave if they cared for their life. That is why the men were very happy that the sun set while they were very far from this cave.

Mogami thought to himself how the person who had sent them to do this work was sitting comfortably at his warm house. "Really, who created chieftaincy?" He introspected. "What makes it possible for one men to exercise command and control to a group of men like this by just one word, with no one questioning him? Why would he command his men to find and force people to fight at the war of strangers? Does he seek to make a better name for himself using the lives of these people? Right now, what wrong has the followers of Motlhaoetla done? Is it wrong to have faith? See, the chief himself is a convert of the church of the whiteman, Dr Ramolaisi. Now he is persecuting followers of Motlhaoetla because he thinks they are taking Dr. Ramolaisi's followers. Is it really a bad thing when someone decides to change his mind and chooses not to believe in a church that is not of Bakwena, chiefs and white people?" Mogami felt the anger burn through his chest but he followed the rest of the men when he could not get answers to his questions.

Chapter 3

As Modiko stayed listening to the sermon he became very happy. He had a form of unusual excitement. It was like that of a man who had just escaped death penalty although he knew he would be faced with life imprisonment. Inside the prison cells at least one still has his life. That is to actually say if living was all about being able to breathe and see things around you. However, that is still not a good life. It is one of a kind that is full of compulsion and has no freedom. The disowning of one's identity is something that is totally not humane at all. He listened carefully to the words that pastor Mmolaaditso said to him and the rest of the baptismal candidates:

"Before I read the baptismal instruction, I want to tell you a very short account," the pastor said immediately after the congregation sang the hymn. They were under a huge mosetlha tree in an open space at Taneele Moithati's home in Gametsimabe. His teeth were sharp and looked like sharp objects used to poke the animal skin. His gums looked like they were plucked into the sharp teeth.

"Once upon a time an evangelist man went to the bush and preached to all animals. Most of the animals were converted and they dedicated their lives to the lord." He continued, "the pig, cow and the goat too were converted and they dedicated their lives to upholding the law. The evangelist was very happy for the conversion of these animals so he gave them a special attire which the animals would wear at heaven. It would have been a true testimony that the animals had given their lives to the lord. Three well-fitting suits were tailored by the evangelist for each one of these animals. The material that was used for the outfit was very expensive and they were tailored very beautifully. 'This is the evidence that you are followers of the Lord and you must take a very good care for these clothes.' The evangelist instructed the animals who replied by saying 'We will take good care of them pastor.' The evangelist then left the animals and went away.

Just before he passed through the nearby river, the goat got bitten by a fly. Instantly it ran and rubbed against a motlhakola tree. Upon realizing that rubbing against the tree did not yield any results, it bleated and rubbed itself desperately against an uneven wall. The suit was left torn apart and worn out.

Since it was very hot, the suit that the pig wore made the situation worse. It advanced towards the pond where it desperately swam in the mud." The pastor mimicked the actions of the pig as all the congregation broke up with laughter. As if not noticing what was happening, he continued: "There were tadpoles and algae on the pond that had just began to dry. So, the mud was still very wet when the pig smeared the suit with the mud. After the mud had dried on the suit, it looked torn and worn out. It was the cow only that took care of the outfit. Upon arrival, the evangelist was extremely discouraged by the behavior of the goat and the pig. He demanded to know why the goat and the pig could not do as the cow did. In response, the pig went back to the mud whereas the goat rushed to the wall once more. The two confessed that that they thought it was a very difficult thing to disown their culture. They even asserted that the new religion was not for animals at all." That's how the pastor concluded his story.

He then looked at those who had just got baptized. His eyes harnessed through them as his cheek shook as if he wanted to laugh. He looked at Modiko for a while because he knew that the school boys who were probably of Modiko's age denied the existence of God. Modiko felt as if he was sitting on top of hellfire. He felt as if God was looking at him. He was lucky however because one of the women in the congregation started singing. The pastor then looked at the hymn book and joined the song.

"Baptism is not a joke as the worldly people may think," the pastor continued afterwards. "When we baptize you, we're actually cleansing you all of your sins so that you get forgiveness instantly. Your sins are therefore left to remain in this river. The water is actually used to cleanse your sins. If you commit transgressions again, your sins will pile up and you will eventually turn out to be a hypocrite. You'd be like a person who does not fear God, one who commits sin like a pig after which he claims that it is his culture. You have to throw away your old ways and never ever think of imitating the pig's behavior. Your old ways are sinful and they are the order of this system of things that is full of transgression.

Tell me this, considering that Jesus did not commit any sin, why did he get baptized?" The pastor asked and focused his sight on those who had been baptized. Silence evaded the place since questions and answers were not allowed in the church service. More importantly such correspondence would be uncalled for during the service of this importance. "The reason was that Jesus had been born by an earthly human being," he responded to the question that he had just asked. "The flesh is very dirty and disgusting. The sin has been part of Adam's flesh after he ate the fruit in the garden of Eden. As a result, everyone who is the son of Adam is a sinner who deserves to burn in hellfire."

Modiko could feel the goosebumps when the pastor mentioned the fire. He even recalled the hot coal that he once stepped on during summer. He could remember the way he was screaming loudly. By then he was still a very young boy and wondered if he could scream in the same way. He thought again about how Modise screamed like a baby when he felt the pain. The thought of this fiery red fire and the scorpions as well as the millipedes which were the size of an elephant frightened him. He was very scared when he thought about the giant man with a long tail and looking like a big baboon as well as the monkeys which had wings of bats. For a minute, his blood froze in his system when he thought about these things. He comforted himself by thinking that he would escape such things because he is now baptized.

At this point, pastor Mmolaaditso was reading a verse that says new beer cannot be poured into old calabashes for they will break and waste that beer. The same scripture says that an old piece of cloth cannot be patched into a new piece of clothing. "These words were said by Jesus himself," he said, as he closed the bible while patting it with his left hand. It was as if he was doing so in order to emphasize his point. "The old calabashes symbolize everyone who does not believe in the Lord. Such people claim that they are followers of tradition. They are cursed sinners. They are going to experience eternal persecution in the unquenchable fire. The new patch cloth and alcohol all have evangelical significance. You are newly born creatures because you have been born again. You are now children of God and not just his ordinary people."

He then read the ten commandments to all those who had been baptized. He instructed them to observe the commandments so that they can have a place in heaven. As he read the commandments slowly, he made sure that he explained each law very clearly and slowly. He made sure that he would explain complex phrases and sentences. However, he spent more time in explaining the commandment which said: "Do not steal. Usually all sinners take advantage of the ambiguity in this commandment because they want to justify their transgressions. Firstly, this commandment may mean that you should not commit theft. Secondly, it may mean that it is thievery to take someone's possession without their consent. That is stealing." As if to make sure that no one misses the point, he repeated the explanation of this commandment. Upon realizing that the older women were already yawning he knew that he had spent too much time speaking. He then came up with a hymn which all the congregation joined in singing. The voice of Evangel Letlotla suppressed the voices of the women who sang the hymn.

Some of the believers went outside one by one to stretch a little bit so that they could stop dozing. After that they came back to the light under mosetlha tree to continue with the service. It was an all-night prayer event which was known as tsoseletso. Its solemn purpose was to reawaken the faith of the believers and strengthen them in their faith. The service had started the previous day after the congregation had shared a meal together. The main idea was to give an elaborate instruction to all those who were newly baptized. Three fire places were set and burning continually so that the congregation was kept warm. At this time of July, winter was at its apex thus counting the number of blankets each man had. A bulb that emitted a reddish light hung from one of the branches of the mosetlha tree. It was this light that the pastor used to read from his bible. "Let there be peace dwelling upon you children of God," said the pastor after the rest of the congregation had sat down.

"Amen," the congregation responded with positive energy.

"I will read a scripture for all of the newly baptized. It is about all the principles that you are supposed to uphold and observe since you are the newly found members of the congregation. In this church of Motlhaoetla, we refrain from doing these things: We do not smoke; we do not marry more than one wife; We get only one wife; We don't drink alcohol; We don't eat the meat from some animals." He then opened the bible and began perusing through its pages pretty rapidly.

"Let us read from the scripture of Leviticus chapter eleven until the Lord stops us." The pastor waited for some time without reading. He wanted to give the older women enough time to open from their bibles. In doing so, each of the old women in the congregation would approximate the bible to the eyes for a better sight. As they searched the referred scripture, they would stick their thumbs to pick some saliva from their tongues so they could open the pages with ease. Some turned their bibles towards the fireplace so that they could take advantage of the light. He began reading after he reckoned that most of them had identified the right scripture, "the scriptures told that the Lord had instructed that only animals with a divided hoof, and ones that chewed the cud such as goats and cows may be eaten. It was forbidden to eat any animal which does not have a divided hoof. The scripture continued to explain that it was unclean to eat pork because, in spite of the fact that its hoof was divided, it did not chew the cud."

That was when Modiko thought of very delicious letlhodi beans which he once had at MmaKebonyemodisa's home. The beans were cooked with fat from the pig and it was extremely delicious! He knew that that was the last time he would have that since he converted. Pastor Mmolaaditso emphasized that the Lord once found a swine of pigs near the sea. He instantly removed the bad spirit form a mad man and put it in the swine. All the pigs then went crazy and drowned themselves in the sea. The pastor emphasized that among all the animals that may be eaten, it was forbidden to eat them when they had blood inside.

"Traditional medicine, traditional beer and that of the whiteman, smoking and traditional dance are all sinful," the pastor continued. After he finished talking, he put the bible on the chair and then asked the congregation to sing a hymn. Evangelist Ramarepetla erupted with a hymn which all the women joined in singing. He sang eloquently like a girl in the traditional dance song and it made an enchanting harmony when the women joined him in singing. The older women's voices lagged behind thus interfering with the tempo of the hymn. When the hymn was just about to finish all the attention of the congregation was shifted to the abrupt and loud cry from one of the women. Her name was Ntshipi. She was the first to get baptized that Saturday morning. The poor woman fell to the ground and when she fell, it sounded like a bone was hitting against a rock. As she cried, she shook her body like a pig that had consumed poison. Some of the elderly women held her and removed her from the middle of the congregation. Immediately, she stopped crying. As she wiped off her tears she declared that there was something that she wished to tell the congregation. Her hands shook, however, as she announced that she had seen a revelation. Women of this congregation were used to seeing such revelations and therefore they instantly brought her before the church. The hymn which had erupted when she was taken out of the church halted. All the eyes were fixed on this woman who earlier on looked shy when she was getting baptized. With confidence and courage, she said: "Peace be with you holy congregation."

"Amen!" the congregation responded. Most members were either looking shocked or amazed.

"I have been sent to tell you that the regiment from the chief is fast approaching. These men will arrest us but we should not fight them back. We should be just submissive to them in the same way as the son of God did to the Jews." She paused for a few seconds. Modiko was very frightened. He was also amazed and wanted to ask who could have said that to the woman. Like a young boy pretending to be asleep while he is listening to the elders discussing their intimate secrets, Ntshipi closed her eyes. She then continued:

"I can see them right now as they are about to cross Moleele river. They are walking very slowly and it is a group of about twenty five men." She stood still for quite some time before she continued, "the Lord says that they will arrive tomorrow at around noon so that they can find us in the middle of the service and catch us red handed." The woman then jumped instantly like someone who is just waking up from a very long slumber. A hymn was sung and the congregation fixed their eyes on this woman as if they were looking at an angel. Pastor Mmolaaditso was the one who later commented that the Lord uses his people to make revelations. He swallowed the scripture that talks about how the young men and virgins would get filled with the holy spirit so that they can prophesy.

****

It was very early in the morning when the leader of the regime woke up his men. "Time is up, men of the chief," he said while shaking some of them to cease their sleep. Let us go and find them while it is morning. It was a very challenging exercise to wake these men up. The coldness of the winter had forced them to coil themselves in an attempt to keep the cold away. The fire that was set before they could sleep was no longer there. It was just some ashes left from the burnt wood. All of them were stretching whereas some kept on sneezing and dozing off their sleep. Their necks and waists were hurting because of the posture they had adopted at night. The leader of the regime then repeated the instructions of the chief so that everything was clear to the men.

"You all remember that Mokwena has instructed that we must arrest Motlhaoetla followers when we find them at church doing against the chief's order that they should stop their worship. It is better to arrive very early at Gametsimabe so that we can find them in the middle of the service. Let us go find them as early as now Bakwena betsho." Just when they started moving, Mogami felt some weight on the right pocket of his jacket. Out of curiosity, he put his hand inside it to find out what could be in his pocket. He felt a very slippery thing. At once he jumped and threw away the beaker which had the beans inside. He screamed loudly like a he-donkey during spring. Using his bare hands, he pulled out the buttons of his jacket, threw it away and stood at a distance while sweating profusely as if it was not cold.

"Man, what's the problem?" One of the men asked with shock.

"It is inside the jacket there!" Mogami screamed again while pointing at his jacket.

"What?" The leader asked. Montsho could not stop laughing upon catching the sight of the abandoned beaker that had kabu beans. He laughed until the tears came out of his eyes as he saw the dark soup of the beans flowing into sandy patches of the soil. One of the men went and turned the jacket and the black mamba came out of the pocket and escaped to the nearby bush. When the other men tried to take the logs of wood to kill the snake, the leader told them that they had to leave because time was up. All this time Montsho couldn't stop laughing until eventually all men joined in the laughter.

"Probably you are the one who put the snake inside Mogami's pocket. Why are you laughing so hard?" One of the men enquired.

"Ehe! The snakes here in Moleele can be carried by hand and put in the pockets. Are they that friendly?" Montsho remarked while he was still laughing.

"Perhaps you Mogami committed some violations before you came here. Why is it that dangerous things happen to you alone? When you have to undertake the regime work, it is very important for a men to refrain from violating some taboos," one of the men said. Like a sheep that is getting slaughtered, Mogami didn't say a word.

All the men left Moleele river, where they had spent the night, and passed through the eastern side of Ramakatlanyane's field. They walked in silence for some time but later they began enquiring from people about the place of Taneele Moithati while they were at Tšhaokeng. None of them knew where Gametsimabe was, and it was very challenging to find the place.

It was during winter and towards the end of July, or the beginning of August. At this time of the season, many people were busy pounding surplus sorghum. Women kept on poking the pumpkins that boys carried in the ox wagons called dilei from the empty field. The cattle, goats and donkeys were all scattered in the field finishing anything that was not harvested. That is why it was crucial to harvest the pumpkins as early as possible to save them from the teeth of the donkeys. Men were idling in each of the homesteads looking for where they could sip some traditional beer. They were also worried about negotiating with the people who had cars to help them carry their sorghum from the fields as they awaited the upcoming rains in the forthcoming year.

In the meantime, the villagers would be eating lengangale in their homesteads to avoid eating all of the sorghum. This was done deliberately so that they don't risk having too few seeds in the next ploughing season. All the sorghum pounding was done as part of molaletsa during the evening. At this time, thicker soft porridge which was prepared from pounded sorghum was cooked in big pots with meat. All the young boys and girls would come in large numbers to be part of the pounding activity. They would be very busy like that until late at night when the food would be served. During such event, the rich would slaughter a lot of goats. Younger boys would be enjoying large portions of the steaks during the molaletsa feast. The following day, all the women would put fill the sacs with some pounded sorghum and then men would take them to places where the surplus food is stored. Usually, all the vehicles that carry the sorghum arrive at night at most of the homesteads. The packing work is deliberately done in the late afternoons so that they can arrive during the night when it is dark. This is done so as to stop witchcraft and to prevent Bakwena from seeing the amount of harvest an individual has. It was also done so because of the fear people had in the chief's tax collectors who would go around during the day to find people who had not yet paid tax. Some of these men could take up to five years without paying tax, and because of this they would hide during the day for they feared being arrested and then sent to jail. It is not darkness only inside the jail that these men feared the most. They also feared the ticks, which are said to be hungry all the time and very strong such that they could only get killed by a bullet.

That's the main reason why these men, upon their arrival in Tshaokeng, encountered a lot of problems in finding their way to Gametsimabe. The men in the regime of Maakathata arrived when the sun was right above their heads and it seemed like wherever they asked for directions all the women they found in the homesteads claimed that they didn't know. In some instances, they would spot a man from a distance but would find out that he had just disappeared into thin air by the time they arrived in the homestead. Everyone in the fields certainly knew that the men came looking for people who had not paid their tax.

After hours of enquiring from about ten households with no results, with not even a single person hinting to them the whereabouts of Taneele Moithati's yard, they resorted to using force against the people. By so doing they were hoping to scare the residents and cause them to panic or else they would loiter for nothing. They could not even see at least one man but it was the women only that they found in the homes. When they set their feet in the next home they became more serious. They spotted a man from a distance but he hid himself and swiftly disappeared into the wall as they approached. After they arrived the leader of the regime enquired about the whereabouts of the man they saw from his wife. "He has since long gone to work for the Whiteman, long, long time before the harvest."

"I saw him running into the house while I was coming this way. What should I do to if I find him inside?" The leader barked.

"I said he's not here. He's gone to work for the white man."

The leader got very furious and lost his temper. His eyes shrinked and looked as if they had been poked with a sharp needle. "Come here so that we can see for ourselves!" He roughly pulled the women into the house as five men from the group followed him.

Due to panic, Serokana—the man who owned the field—tried to hide under the bed. Unfortunately, his legs were left exposed outside because he went under the bed with his head first. His old pair of shoes that he wore were just in the open space. It was even easier to spot the dark mud that had dried on the shoe.

"Now what is this? Isn't it your husband hee?" The leader fumed with the kind of anger a python would usually have at the sight of barking dogs. "So, your husband left his legs behind when he left for Gauteng? Are you intending to play funny?"

"No…. he went using Thepa's car and he didn't walk there." The woman was so scared that she didn't even know how to say what she wanted to say. She said her response in desperate confusion. All the five men broke with abrupt laughter. They pulled Serokana from underneath the mattress like a chicken being pulled out from very heavy branches. He was bleeding from the scratch he had got in his face while he was trying to hide. He was very scared that his eyes were wide open for a long time. He shook like a dry leaf responding to the effect of the whirlwind. Although the church leader was very angry he felt compelled to feel sorry for him. He then asked him with a soft soft voice.

"What is your name?"

"I'm Serokana sir"

"Okay Serokana, come outside—there are a few questions that I'd like you to answer." Serokana nearly had a heart attack when they got outside. A group of men sat outside waiting for him. He was shaken and terrified upon catching the sight of this mob of men, who were probably more than twenty in number. Some were even sitting on top of his yard wall. They all had their eyes fixed on him just like a wild cat would do to a rat. One of the men was already enjoying a piece of grilled pumpkin that had been prepared for Serokana to eat. Serokana felt sorry for himself. He could feel the sweat dripping all the way from his neck down to the waist. He finally gave up into believing that he will pay the price of whatever comes his way. His wife and children wept silently for they feared provoking the anger of the mob. The men in the regime had a reputation of spanking anyone who crosses them, more especially if they had to spend a long time before they find that individual. They would never hesitate to use a thick stick to bitterly whip someone on their buttocks.

Serokana had stayed up to five years without paying tax which was about a pound per year. By then it was a lot of money. His tartered pants looked very old and had numerous patches both inside and outside that it was very confusing to tell what kind of trousers he wore. It was only when he began to wet his pants that the leader felt sorry in seeing how terrified Serokana was. He then said: "Serokana, we know it's been a couple years without paying tax but that's fine. Everyman always has some violations, otherwise if not he is considered to be a

31

boy, is that not so?" He smiled continually as he patted him on his shoulder like a boy would do upon seeing his lover. He then went on.

"Don't get used to show your agreement by nodding like that Serokana. Man, we're looking for the followers of Motlhaoetla church. We've been told that they are at Taneele Moikgatlhi's place."

"Taneele Moithati!" One of the men from the group corrected him.

"Taneele Moithati Rra, I almost got lost. If you could just show us where Moithati's place is we will leave you in peace, without causing you any affliction." He looked at Serokana in the eyes and he saw how he now felt a lot more relaxed. He sighed loudly and smiled quietly.

There were sputters of white clouds in the sky that looked bluish with a few glimmering red colors. The powerful winds picked the red dust and dead grass which sat on the men's faces as they advanced towards Mmasebele which was way further from Gametsimabe. Every now and then the birds would sing continually from either the clear sky or trees whose leaves have dried due to winter. Now, after Serokana realized that the men had passed Gametsimabe after walking for many miles, he asked for permission to be allowed to go back. He claimed that he did not want to be burnt with fire by the God of Motlha-o-Etla church. The leader and the rest of the men in his regime were not suspecting him so they immediately let him free.

"Return with peace the big crocodile. May your ancestors go with you and break the sharpness of the sticks," responded the leader.

On his way back, Serokana knew that if the men found out that he had misled them, he would have to pay a painful price. He well knew that the men were going to deal with him sarcastically. Because of this, he began to pace very fast thus leaving gullies of footprints as he ran like an athlete who did not want to lose a marathon. He unearthed the rocks on the ground with all the energy he had. The pair of shoes that he wore were worn out and they had a metallic sole. This is the very pair that he used while he worked at the mine. They were completely destroyed on the side but in spite of this he used them to rip apart the dry ground as he ran for his life. Immediately he decided that he would not go to his home. He'd rather go to Gakgatla where he anticipated to spend a night and return the following day when the situation was better.

On their arrival, the men of the regime found a very old man with white beard in one of the compounds which they had been shown. He used the leaf from mosetlha tree to keep flies away from bothering him. A small boy who had been instructed to go and hide the skull of the sheep which the old man had been enjoying before he saw the men sat next to him. The old man had sent this young boy to hide it when he heard the barking of the dogs. His beard was green around the nostrils due to frequent sniffing of the snuff. All the men salivated as they smelled the mutton that had since evaded the place. After they greeted him, he covered his face with his palm, as if he is protecting sunrays from entering his eyes. He then asked, "Who is your father boys?" They explained that they were a regime from the chief and they had been sent to arrest the converts of Motlhaoetla church.

"But why are you looking for them in this side of Diphephe? Isn't it that these people hold their prayers in Gametsimabe?" The old man charged with evident irritation. It was very clear that he was appalled by this church, since he believed that it destroyed the traditional Setswana ways. He had spent the whole day without a proper meal because all of his children had gone to this church. Even traditional beer was no longer brewed at home because it was considered a sin by the church. He could only have a sip of the beer after he had gone a very long distance to find where it was brewed. He explained all this to the rest of the men before he enquired why they had passed Gametsimabe. Before any of them could reply he interrupted: "Perhaps you are coming here with some sort of conspiracy? You know all of you younger people are just crooks. But this cleverness will never protect you."

The leader explained to him that they spent the entire day searching but the villagers were refusing to show them Taneele Moithati's home. He also told him about Serokana. He bowed his head a little bit before he spit a bit of saliva on the ground. He then covered the spit with his shoe which had a sole made of the tire from a modern car. "You see! This is what I just told you earlier about the foolish tricks that you

33

young people have. Instead of showing you the way to help you get rid of the dragon that is killing our ways and our people, he would rather mislead you?"

He kept quiet for a minute because of the anger that ran through his veins. The men retraced their steps after the old man gave them directions. Each of one of them was swearing that wherever they would find Serokana, they would definitely show him his mother. It was at around the late afternoon when the men arrived at Gametsimabe. They entered through the same compound which they had passed when they were advancing from Tšhaokeng. They called out the person who was busy making noise with the dishes inside the house. A young boy finally came out of the house while wiping his tiny lips. He greeted them.

"Boy, do you know where Taneele Moithati's compound is?" Montsho asked. "Are you refering to Taneele, the one who herds Radipela' cattle?" All the men looked confused. They then knew that it would be easier if they call Taneele using his child's name. The boy was completely lost, he was thinking of another young boy. "How old is he?" Montsho asked again but the boy asked who the man was talking about.

"The same Taneele that you are talking about, your sister's buttocks!" Montsho screamed to the young boy with fury. The boy was very frightened that whatever he said was senseless and didn't help the men arrive at what they wanted. One of the men noticed the whiteness of the sugar that had stuck at the boy's chin. He then realized that use of force would not give any positive result. They had just been derailed because they used compulsion. He fondly drew close to the boy and lowered his tone softly. He immediately put his hand in the pocket and came with some sugar, which he gave the young boy to enjoy. "My child, please tell me this, where is the gathering place for Motlhaoetla church? Where do you always hear people chanting hymns?" As he talked, he gave more of the sugar to the boy.

At once the little boy tasted the sweetness of the sugar and then showed the men the right direction without hesitation: "After you pass

34

that gate and then you proceed further to Mmatlhalejaphala, that is where the church gathers."

The man gave more sugar to the boy before they parted ways. When the little boy arrived home, he met his mother who was at that time coming from fetching some water. His mother asked him where he got the sugar and the boy narrated the whole story with all the excitement he had. After he told his story, she hit him very hard at the back using her fist. "You sold children of God with sugar? You Judas Iscariot!" The woman yelled.

The men, who were at a distance this time were shocked to hear their friend crying loudly. They found Taneele Moithati's compound filled with worshipers and the service was being led by Evangelist Letlotla. When they arrived, it was as if they had been expected since there was no sign of fear or discomfort when the men engulfed those who had gathered.

At that point, the evangelist realized that the arrival of the chief's men had incited some fear among some of the believers, especially women. Some of the women and men kept looking side by side with their eyes open and their lips dead dry with fear. One could easily pick their fright rom the look of the eyes and the shaking hands. The small children too started crying until their weep swept through the church like a fire that is responding to the provocative wind. After some time, the noise had increased such that it was difficult to hear the words of the evangelist who was now screaming loudly as if he was talking to people who were very far. Discomfort grew among the people in the congregation as they glimpsed the serious faces these men wore. The men had sticks, machetes and axes in their hands but in fact there were just two or three axes only. The machetes were held with the delicacy of a hunter whose attention is fixed on an animal. Their hair was very dirty and it appeared as if they had never ever brushed their teeth in their lifetime. The hair was uncombed and looked frustrated due to sleepless night they had had. Some of the lips of the men were bleeding whereas others were very dry because of the cold. Every now and then a red tongue would appear from one of the men to wipe away the dryness that was rampant in the periphery of their lips. Their faces were now pale and the ears had been obviously withered by the chill of July.

It was then that Evangelist Letlotla realized that the Lord's flock had been surrounded by jackals. He thought it necessary to do something that would re-energize the flock. He felt as if all of the blood in his body ran to his head. His ears opened up but his eyes widened a little bit. He felt his mind stabilizing like the body of water in a stream. At once he said: "Children of God, let us all look to our Lord Jesus in prayer and none of you should keep quiet." He fell on his knees as he talked. The believers started praying with a unified spirit. The mixture of their voices could easily be confused to that of toads and frogs after the first rains. The masculine voices roared like those of male baboons inside the caves while those of women and younger boys were like the cry of a troublesome child.

At first all the men in the group started laughing at this scene, but after a short while each of them became very serious. They even knelt with those gathered at the church without even noticing it. A few of them even started to pray along with the congregation as time went on. Immediately two of the men from this group started crying like children. As the congregation stood up, Evangel Letlotla was rather shocked to discover that two of the men were bowing just by his side, crying continually like no one's business. He instantly noticed what these men wanted and that's when he started to address the congregation: "The time will come in which the wicked will die in the fiery fire which cannot be tried by using one's finger. There will be weeping and gnashing of teeth. Repent therefore, and flee from the upcoming rage!" He glanced at the rest of the men.

"I need the Lord, I am repenting my sins," one of these two men said. It was Mogami and the other men wept bitterly such that he couldn't even speak. The evangelist approached them and then proceeded to lay his hands upon them. At once, the leader of the regime jumped when he saw that his men had been converted to Motlhaoetla. He screamed like a man who had lost all of his family in death: "Mogalammakapaa!!! How am I going to explain this to the chief?" Like a kid whose candy has been taken he put his hands on his head. They then walked the rest of the believers to Molepolole.

Chapter 4

Doctor Clifford Lovelace removed his white coat and the stethoscope which he frequently used whenever duty called. He put them on top of the table and then hung the coat on the wall. After that he walked to his apartment. His house was a good distance away from the place where patients slept. A small room which was primarily used as the change room for doctors sat next to a line of the patient dorms. In front of this building, there was a big mosu tree and further to this tree there was another huge morolwana tree. All the corridors of the building had the green corrugated iron roof top that looked the same with the rest of the roof. The floor was painted in deep red color which looked exactly like the blood from an open wound. Every morning, Madalambijana would shine the floor before he goes to chop firewood at doctor Lovelace's house.

Doctor Lovelace opened the door of his house which had the surf that was used to keep flies away. He immediately got enraged even more when he heard the door making a lot of noise from friction. He overturned like an arrogant bull that that seeks to warn a boy from holding its tail. He slammed the door with all his energy and then marched to the back of the house. His green eyes shrunk a little bit before he screamed: "Jack!"

"Rra! oh, my master!" Madalambijana responded. In actuality, his name was not Jack; he was given this name because the white man could not pronounce his name properly.

"Why didn't you put grease in the door? What did I tell you this morning?" He fumed in a very strong accent of Setswana. Madalambijana, a roughly fifty years old man, looked much more like a younger boy due to his height and mental state. He quickly abandoned the axe which he was busy using to chop wood at that time. He removed the hat from his head and rubbed it through his hands with the humility of a guilty dog. Probably one that is dealing with the guilt of eating eggs. "I was still watering the plants and vegetables my lord. I was going to—"

"Shut up bloody Motshwana!" Doctor Lovelace interrupted him in English. His red lips shook with rage. His long nose looked like the sharper side of the knife used to cut pumpkins. It was very thin and looked as if it could be used as a pencil on the paper.

Madalambijane left and then got the grease from its tin and used it to lubricate the door. The doctor used the back door and found Flora cooking in the kitchen. He did not greet her, he opened the cupboard before he went to his bedroom. He jumped on to the bed, removed his shoes and then lied on top of the bed. The bedding was done very well. It had been decorated using a yellow cloth which covered most of the blankets. His wife's bed too was neatly done. It was covered with a cloth that had red and white flowers. A wedding picture of him and Anne hung on the wall by wife's bedside.

"I wouldn't be lonely like this if my wife was here with me." He thought to himself as he lay on the bed with his legs spread. "Well it is just three weeks and she'll be here. I'm pretty sure that she will have a lot to share from home." He wondered for a few minutes, imagining how it looked like since he left fifteen years back. He had left when he was about thirty. That was after he had completed his medical and pastoral studies. He had come to Africa with the objective of civilizing a black man. He had been told that these people stay on trees just like baboons. He never forgot the story of a baboon that was brought by sailors in London. It was believed that this baboon was an African. When he arrived in Africa, he found humans, although they were not civilized according to his conception. However, they were not at all like baboons. According to his, at least there wasn't much of a difference between black people and baboons.

"The only distinction between a baboon and black man is that the baboon has more fur. The fur in black man has been withered by the clothes that we gave him to wear. But when it comes to brain and skin color, they are just one family," he explained to the newly arrived John Cloud, who was to work as the chief district officer for Kweneng region.

Florah hesitated to knock at the door. "Tea is ready doctor" She said. "I'll come mma. Thank you," he responded with an accent.

Doctor Lovelace stood up from his bed. He then stretched his arms, coughed, and then went to the kitchen. In the kitchen, a cup of tea sat next to the bread that was smeared with butter. He once again boiled with anger as if his heart had choked his throat. This was the third time he had told Florah that she must always bring butter and all the other things on a plate. He would take care of the smearing himself. He almost tore his nostrils sighing so loudly that Florah could hear him from the kitchen. She didn't say anything though. Inside his heart, he concluded that it was impossible to educate Motswana. The military horses were way much better because they could be trained for war tactics. The dogs could be tamed to help police and even shepherd the flock. But it will take water to come from a rock in carrying the exercise of teaching Motswana until he fully understands.

He put some sugar in his tea and then stirred it after which he tasted it. It was well done. He smiled with some excitement as he thought of the day when Florah was still new to her job. She did something that extremely angered him. However, from then that was to become the funny story of his life. It was about three years ago, just before his wife left for England to complete her intensive midwifery studies. That time he was with Anne when Florah brought tea in the evening. While they were still talking Florah added some sugar for them, stirred it and then tasted if it was sweet enough using the teaspoon. All this tea was disposed because she had put the teaspoon back into the cup. She was forced to make tea again. Lovelace never forgets this incident and he laughs every time he thinks of it. That morning before he went for duty break at around ten, he got appalled by one of the nurses.

Chapter 5

The morafe started to gather at around morning time, probably at the time when the cattle would go to the river. The whole village was full of life and commotion just like termites on the anthill. Those who were coming from distant places such as the Bokaa clan had started walking very early in the morning. Men and women swayed to the direction of the Kgotla so as to witness for themselves the fate that was to befall the worshipers of Motlha-o-Etla church. It had been known across the village that the worshipers had been arrested after they were seen being led like cattle. Because of this happening, the rest of the villagers went to the Kgotla leaving behind children and the blind.

Tlholego the old man placed his pipe on top of the wall. He then went inside the house to take his jacket since that day he woke up late when it was a little warm. He drew from the casket a goat horn which was full of dark medicine inside. He used his pointing figure to take some of the medicine and then applied it to his forehead and then on the joints. After that he covered the horn and put it back in the casket drawer. He took a red root, took a bite and spit to the front. He took another bite, spit to the back and then to the sides and said:

"My ancestors, my forefathers, kill the sharpness of the thorns and put them to sleep." He said goodbye to his wife who was at the back of the yard.

"I am going to the chief's place to witness the judgment of the worshippers."

"Ehe rra, go with ancestors Mokwena! I am not feeling well otherwise I could be going there too," she responded.

Rre Tlholego threw the jacket on his shoulders. He put some tobacco in his pipe and used his thumb and pointing finger to pick a glowing coal. He held it for quite some time before he put it on the pipe. He inhaled the pipe so that after about two puffs a cloud of smoke which came from his nostrils formed in the air. He then took the glowing coal and threw it back on the fire before he proceeded to leave the yard. This two fingers which he used to hold the hot coal were now almost dead because of doing that all the time. He wore his coat and went to his friend's home in Maribana clan. Upon arrival he found Maribana almost leaving through the gate.

"Truly speaking you are such a selfish person! Why is it that when you see me you hit the road?" Rre Tlholego asked.

"What on earth have you yourself ever given me to eat at your house? I am a fast and energetic boy. I am not like you, who wakes up very late." Rre Mokgaodi charged back and the two men laughed.

"Let's stop by home so that you can greet the children. You will do that just standing so that we can hurry to the other side of the village," Rre Mokgaodi said as he turned back, tracing his steps back into his home. "But how are you son?... the upper side"

"Wai! It is just one of a kind that is only expressed verbally, using the mouth while in the actual fact my health is not that good. How about yourself, son of Kweneng? I can see you are doing quite well health-wise," Rre Tlholego asked as they entered the home.

Rre Mokgaodi's grandchild came with a chair and put it next to where his grandfather had sat. "It is not my intent to sit down today my grandchild, I was just stopping by for greetings. I'm in much of a hurry." Rre Tlholego said after he greeted the old woman. She asked if Rre Tlholego was not even going to sip some traditional beer of which he declined and said that they really had to hurry. Then they left with Rre Mokgaodi.

"You said I appear to be in good health, but can't you see how worn out I am? I want to go where my ancestors went," Rre Mokgaodi added. "You young men are the ones who will continue to live, whereas we are aging and of course very tired."

"Ag! Just die! You have had a large portion of your share on planet earth. Give chance for others. Unless if you wanted to be like the grave that long ate our grandfathers but until now it doesn't get satisfied?"

Now, these two old men were age mates. The only difference was that Rre Mokgadi was born during winter and Rre Tlholego was born in the following winter. Otherwise they belonged to the same mophato or regiment of Masitaoka. As they went forth to the chief's place, Rre Tlholego noticed some smoke coming out of Rre Mokgadi's pocket.

"These tobacco that gets smoked by young boys, see there, your jacket is burning." Rre Mokaodi then put his hand in the pocket and compressed the piece of cloth that was burning. Rre Tlholego continued:

"Maybe you are burning your jacket because you feel the warmth of this morning's weather. You know that this month that has just started is called tebatsabarwaledi, at night the cold will be plucking a tick and a bug."

Before Rre Mokgaodi could even reply, a group of men greeted them. They joined them and walked until they all arrived at the Kgotla. The place was packed but the chief was not there yet, so the work of tormenting the Motlha-o-Etla worshipers had not started yet. The villagers came from almost every part of the village. A brief exchange of greetings would be done before one could sit on the stump or the chair they would have brought from their home. As for most of young men, they saw dust because even if they had brought chairs for themselves they were forced to surrender them when an elderly men came without a chair. That's why when Rre Tlholego and Rre Mokgaodi arrived, young men who had brought chairs had to stand up. This two old men sat by the sides of the poles which were facing the sun.

At the heart of the Kgotla there was a very big fire place. Towards the Kgotla center, perhaps near the pillars there were worshipers of Motlha-o-Etla. These included men, women and children. Most of women and children had shrunk themselves due to last night's cold. All the villagers who had come to witness this event had surrounded the area as if they were a kraal and only left a small space between them and the worshipers. On the other space stood men from the regime who had been sent to arrest worshipers of Motlha-o-Etla. After they arrested them at Gametsimabe, the men made sure that they paced the worshipers to ensure they arrived in the village before sunset. As such, despite darkness they arrived in Molepolole when it was still easy to identify a person who walks in the dark from a distance.

Women, children and the elderly got exhausted from walking at such a pace but evangel Letlotla kept encouraging them with these words: "Those who get persecuted in the name of the Lord will get salvation." He even added that persecution in these times is way much better compared to the one that occurred before the war. He said that by then they were led using horses not by fellow walking human beings.

As they entered the village, villagers from the homes next to the road stood up by the fence to see for themselves. Even some men who were drinking tswidi left it for some time so that they could witness this event properly. The worshipers spent the entire night at the Kgotla, watched carefully by the mophato as if they were thieves awaiting a trial.

Most of the worshippers were coughing because of the cold they were exposed to all night. Some of them had runny and stuffy noses because of the flu they caught. There was a very loud noise from the rest of the villagers who kept pointing at the worshipers in their talk. Shortly thereafter the chief arrived. He was followed by his younger brother and his uncles. They were all very fat men, considerably big. As always, their ears were exactly those from kweneng—they were spread apart like a toy car made of wires or the dried covers of a melon. At once all of the village rose up as if they were just one person.

After the chief and his men took their positions, there was a pause of silence for some time until the chief said;

"I am greeting you Bakwena let the rain fall on you!"

"Pula! Let it rain Mmabatho."

The chief and his advisors sat down and his seat faced a pillar that was bigger than others. A minute of silence passed for a few seconds. The men who wore hats pulled them to their eyes as if they were being troubled by the sunlight. However, in this state they looked more stubborn and gigantic. They appeared as people who hated lawlessness, lovers of fellow men, traditionalists and people who stood to protect nature and old ways. For some time, the gathering place looked as if it was a correctional place for people who fought against violence and those who supported good civilization. It looked as if it were a sieve used to filter any form of unruly conduct against civilization of mankind. After a while, the chief's brother, whom they fondly named Ponto-le-šeleng for he always referred to 'Pound and Shilling' when he judged cases, stood up. After greeting the chief and the villagers, he said:

"Mokwena, I know that you are already here for the hearing of those who are to be tried. Where are the people who went to arrest them? Where is the leader of Maakathata?"

"I'm here my lord," the leader said while standing up and bending his hat at the same time.

"Then go ahead and give the chief a report of how you went and what you are bringing here."

The leader went to the front and all this while he continually cuddled his hat. He then bowed and said: "Mmabatho!" He sat straight and pulled his jacket to its place but after using his tongue to lick his lips which had been dried by hunger he continued.

"In short and very briefly I may say we went and arrived at the place where Mokwena had sent us. We experienced some hardships at Tšhadibeng…Montsho was it at Tšhadibeng at that place?" He asked as he looked at the side where Montsho sat.

"Tšhaokeng!" one of the men from the regime corrected him. Montsho nearly had a heart attack as he thought that the leader would mention that he fought with Mogami as he had threatened.

"At Tšhaokeng my master. People at that place were scared to tell us where Gametsimabe was. We met a lot of hardships until we finally arrive at Gametsimabe." He also reported what Serokana did to them by sending them to a wrong direction. When he summed up his speech, he said:

"We finally found the worshippers of Motlha-o-Etla worshipping underneath mosetlha tree at Taneele Moikgatlhi's compound, kgae! I meant to say Taneele Moithati not Moikgatlhi my lord. Taneele stand up so that they can see you. Where is he? Stand up!"

Taneele Moithati stood from the masses of the worshipers with his chest out. His balding skull shone like a mirror left in the morning sun.

He was lighter in complexion but also very short. His beard was very huge like that of a he goat and it blanketed the rest of his cheeks.

"Sit down because Mokwena has seen you." The leader commanded. He bumped himself to the ground with his buttocks like a school boy.

"We found them on the service and praying against your will my lord. All those who are here my lord are the ones we caught red-handed. We however left all those who had gone to the bush or those who had gone to take a piss. Our forefathers have a saying that we only shoot at a rat that is basking, but one that is on the branches…" He spread his hands, "There was a few women who had gone out to stop their babies from crying. Although they troubled us and claimed that they too were part of the worshipers we refused to arrest them for a thief is one who gets caught red-handed. So here they are my master." He bowed and pulled his pants so as to stop it from falling to the knees and then sat down.

The chief's brother stood up, looked at the chief and said:

"This is the report, the great Crocodile. These people who preach peace are continuing to destroy your people. Even if you try to inculcate your command into their ears they don't listen." Ponto-le-šeleng took his seat and his mouth looked as if two plates had been put together.

The chief remained silent for some time. Ever since he returned from the German war, his soul has never rested. Before he went to the war, his brutality to worshippers of these small churches was known by his people. But now there is only one thing that troubles his heart: it is all the men who went to the war. It seems like war has gotten to their heads. These men are very stubborn and they no longer respect chieftaincy like they used to. The only thing that is left in their hearts is harshness from the war. Most of them when they arrived from the war found out that the cowards who were too scared to go the British and German war had messed up with their homes. As a result, they blamed the chief for forcing them to sacrifice their lives at a war which was not theirs.

Now some of these worshippers of Motlha-o-Etla were men who had gone to the war. They might humiliate him in front of his people. The chief's brother was actually the one who had compelled the chief to destroy the worshipers, and take them where the locust went. The chief came back from his engrossed thoughts and found his people waiting for the brutality that he was to bestow upon the worshipers. He looked at them. He noticed that there was not even a sign of fright on the faces of Letlotla and Mmolaaditso. Like people who are used to being persecuted they looked relaxed like a middle aged ass. He looked at his brother and saw his puffy chicks as if he had tasted a poorly brewed traditional beer. He then started talking:

"Why have you continued with your prayers when I have clearly commanded you not to? Are you despising me?"

He looked at Letlotla and Mmolaaditso and then the rest of the congregation. Letlotla stood up to respond but the chief stopped him. He lost his temper more especially because he had had issues with Letlotla. This evangel, apart from being a member of the church that all Bakwena went to, agitated the chief by building a house with a corrugated iron roofing just like the chief himself. He is making himself the chief. So, the people who came to the village could easily get lost and think that Letlotla's home is where the chief lived. The chief decided to let his brother and the uncles handle this case and the judgment started.

Chapter 6

"There they are sir, since you think I am not giving them enough punishment," the chief said as he stood up to go to his house.

At once his brother stood up from the chair with pride and then faced the believers. He repeated the chief's question of why they have continued with their prayers when the owner of the soil they are stepping on has commanded their church to stop. He was very dark in complexion because he was a heavy drinker. His ears looked as if they were pumpkin covers that had been cut by a lazy person. They were separated from the head and were easily shaken by wind. Again, Letlotla stood up to respond.

"Mokwena we are not in any way despising the chief and we are not being hard headed like a he-goat. Really what is wrong about worshipping God?"

"Which God? And in whose land do you pray him? Who gave you the permission to do that and on whose soil are you doing that? Don't you know that the chief can send you on exile from his land?" The chief's brother yelled with his rusty voice.

"The God that we worship is the one who owns this earth, he is even the owner of the soil that you are talking about. He is the one who granted us the permission to pray. Let me read for you from…" Evangel Letlotla talked as he tried to open from the bible. Ponto-le-šeleng interrupted him and commanded the rest of the men from the regime to confiscate all the religious literature that the worshipers had. They were to burn on the fire at the heart of the Kgotla.

After some time, the fire was flaming and the ashes from the burnt pages of the books flew across the pillars of the Kgotla. That was where the trial ended because Ponto-le-šeleng did not allow for any questions. He then ordered that the worshippers should be led to the pillars at the back of the Kgotla. After that he ordered that they should be brought one by one. The first one to be brought before Ponto-le-šeleng and his uncles was Pastor Keitumetse Mmolaaditso.

"Man, why do you keep misleading people with these funny churches? Denounce before this court that you will never worship at Motlha-o-Etla," Ponto-le-šeleng demanded.

"I cannot forsake my Lord even if you kill me," Mmolaaditso replied slowly.

"Senwamoro give him four strokes," one of the chief's uncles ordered. Senwamoro came with his kubu and he kept on straightening it using fat from the sheep. He was known very well and feared. All men started to respect him from the time he flogged a Mokgalagadi man who had stolen the chief's cattle. In fact, this poor man had not stolen them, he had intoxicated them with some tobacco because he was a hungry man. The chief didn't give him food to eat while he took care of his cattle so he thought it better to kill them with tobacco. By the time Bakwena realized this, they swore that he would be an example to the rest of his people. Senwamoro was asked to give him four strokes, or four breasts of a cow as they call it. He stood on his feet with his toes and slashed this poor Mokgalagadi man until blood pumped out of his back like milk coming out of the tits of a cow. When this poor man from the dryland stood up from the ground he was in gross pain. He struggled to pick his piece of clothing made of animal skin and when he was yonder he looked at the men in the Kgotla and insulted them. They all broke into laughter but one of them ordered that this Mokgalagadi man should be given two more strokes. One of the men said, "Just leave him, he is doing that because he feels the pain of the cane."

Now Senwamoro took a kubu and walked toward the pastor who was already lying on the ground with his fat belly. He pounced on him and slashed the first one. The skin was left torn apart and showing white meat which was followed by blood. The pastor oscillated on the ground like a bull feeling the pain of castration. Some people from the masses were laughing, leaving the roof of their mouths exposed. Someone from the audience shouted, "Pastor those are the tithes too."

Senwamoro continued to wallop him with the second one until the last flog and all this while he took some time, to cause the pain to strike and settle deep in the heart. By the time he stood up from the ground, his face was dusty and dry like a child who was being told that his mother had died. Ponto-le-šeleng asked him again if he would continue ignoring the chief's command to which he replied that as long as his soul lives he will never cease praying. After that, Ponto-le-šeleng ordered that the pastor should be made to stand on one feet and that was done.

The second one to come was evangel Letlotla. He explained that only death is the one that could stop him from praying when asked if he was going to stop. It was not his lucky day for as he was speaking the chief arrived from his house.

"Listen to this dog! People, hear what he is saying! What did you say?" They yelled at him like a baby. "Did you say you will never stop praying on my soil? Okay then step out of my soil! Do that at once! Go now to heaven to the God of pastors! Senwamoro, tell him to step out of my soil!"

Senwamoro didn't waste time—he whipped him on his limps and head.

"Monna! This is my soil and you are my dog. Your ticks are servants of my ticks. Your mice are servants of mine. Your father is my father's dog, you are my dog. The rats in your branches are slaves of those which are in my branches. Do you understand that? Who do you think you are that you can pray in my land without my permission? Senwamoro give him strokes the same number as the toes of the feet."

Senwamoro tore him apart with his kubu. The evangelist moaned with pain like an asthma patient during a windy day. After he finished, he still maintained that no matter what he'd rather die praying. Just like they did to the pastor, Ponto-le-šeleng ordered that he should be made to stand on one leg. He also told them that he could only let them sit down if they denounce their faith.

The worshipers kept on coming to Ponto-le-šeleng one by one and most of the women said that they would never do it. Those who had denounced their faith were let free however some of the women refused. They too were ordered to lie on the ground with their backs exposed and they were flogged four strokes each. Pastor Ramarepetla looked on restlessly when he saw the whip dripping blood of believers who had refused to denounce their religion.

One of the chief's uncles, who had not taken the position of the chief's brother since he had gone to the bush repeated the question:

"Rra wee! Are you deaf? I am asking you if you would stop praying with the people of Motlha-o-Etla? Yes or No. It's a question so answer."

"I will never go with them… kgae…I will never break the command of the chief." They let him go and he mixed with the people who had come to see the affliction of the believers.

There were two men in front of Modiko. These two had previously been part of the mophato that the chief had sent to arrest the believers but they got converted. They were brought at the same time. Ponto-le-šeleng who had come back from the bushes looked at them and ordered Senwamoro to give them two lashes before he could ask them any questions. He then asked them:

"What is this nonsense that I hear about you?" Both men looked at each other briefly before Mogami started talking.

"Mokwena, I am very tired of afflicting these poor people of God even though they have not done anything wrong. I thought it was better for me to be persecuted than to turn myself into a monster and consume humans. I think your chieftaincy is now out of order because it is dividing the people instead of uniting them. I suggest that it would be best if your kingdom could…."

"Shut up! Who do you think you are because when men fought for this land you went to botsetsi? You think chieftaincy is all about that? Who are you to teach me about chieftaincy when I myself am a chief?" Ponto-le-šeleng barked.

After that, he didn't ask them anything but ordered that they should be made to go and stand on one feet like others. Modiko was the one who was next. He was wearing a small shirt and short pants. When he stood in front of Ponto-le-šeleng he saw a blue flame when he slapped him in the face. Before he could express his shock, he got another heavy slap on the cheek. He even wetted his khaki pants even though it was not raining. He spent some time idling on thoughts as a pool of tears flew from his eyes the way water flows on the sand of Metsimotlhabe River. When the tears dried from his eyes, he saw a gigantic man standing in front of him and a group of old men from the royalty. He looked both sides and found realized that his mother was not in the masses.

"Mosimane?" Ponto-le-šeleng called. It was a both a question and a commandment.

"Rra!"

"What is your name?"

"I am Modiko."

"Are you a herd boy or you go to school?"

"I go to school."

"Now what are you doing in the middle of the elders? Who did you leave your school work with?"

"School starts tomorrow Rra, so I will be going then."

Now it was as if Ponto-le-šeleng was a father talking to his son without any tension between them. However, immediately Ponto-le-šeleng's eyes turned cold like that of a murderer. They turned red like stones from a red soil. Using his finger that had a broken nail to point at Modiko, he said:

"My child, I have the authority to send you to jail for the rest of your life, but I also have the right to let you go freely. Do you understand clearly the child of my wife?"

"I'm listening Rra!"

"Now I want you to go to school, get educated and become our savior in the future. I want you to be able to interpret English for us when it doesn't fit in our ears. This thing that you are doing is a delinquent behavior and it also despises the chief's rule. It is very bad. Will you ever do this again my boy? Will you ever worship with the lunatics of Motlha-o-Etla against the chief's will?"

Modiko looked at the side where his father, Letlotla stood on one leg. He noticed that his father was looking at him. When he looked at his father's eyes he saw some sparks of light like that of a red lightening of matlakadibe rain. He started thinking. He felt the sun rays of June settling on his shoulders and passing through the ribs and the chest.

"Are you going to denounce the Lord?" His conscience questioned him. In short, he dreaded when that thought visited him. It always kept on coming back to his memory. He saw a man with a tail and hairy hands. Yes! He could see that red flame mixed with yellow color of yolk from a chicken egg. Millipedes about the same size as elephants, centipedes, fuming fires and people's eyes blasting in the fire like popcorn...

"I'm waiting. Give me an answer!" Ponto-le-šeleng barked.

Modiko thought that the canes, jail, and persecutions were much better compared to what he saw in that dreadful vision. "A cane has killed a rat only." He concluded and then responded:

"Rra I fear the Lord more than you. I fear Jesus more than I fear you. As such I will continue worshiping him and denounce your rule Mokwena."

The people covered their mouths with their hands for they did not expect such an insult from a sixteen year old lad. How can an infant that is still smelling of its mother's milk say that to the chief? This was unbelievable because men wet their pants when they appear before the chief. Some people were very amazed that they nearly fainted. Rre Tlholego spit some saliva and used his shoe to cover it. The world has come to an end indeed!

Ponto-le-šeleng was crossed like a male skank. He was so pissed that he feared he might collapse and for this he sent one of the men to bring him some cold water. He felt better after drinking some water. He ordered that this fatherless boy must be given strokes the same number as the breasts of a pig and then let free. Senwamoro didn't waste time, he destroyed his skin with a cane. After he was finished with him the boy couldn't even stand up. One of the royal henchmen who stood from a distance said:

"Get back to him and give him another one so he stops lying as if he was a snake."

Senwamoro pounced on him with another stroke but the boy remained motionless still, just like a piece of cloth.

The chief freaked when he thought that some men who went to the war might influence morafe about this inhumane deed. He thought of a story which his father told him that his great grandfather once got beaten by his people because of brutal persecution like this. He ordered that the boy should be taken to the chief's house.

As for Ponto-le-šeleng, he was happy about this because he thought it would serve as an example to the rest of the believers who come from the small churches that it is uncalled for to ignore the chief's command. After all the worshipers were questioned and tried, those who had stood on one leg for time felt the pain on their knees and a few of them chose to denounce their faith so that they could be let to sit down. Letlotla and his other folks remained standing. All those who had refused to denounce their faith were sent to jail according to the order of the chief. Those who came late were told and shown what happened except that it was coupled with some lies.

The chief warden entered the jail after some time and rebuked the prisoners at once like a male baboon. Silence enveloped the place. The believers had started singing just after they entered the cell. He gazed at them the same way a cock would do to a scorpion—with a full knowledge that it had the power to pierce its body with its hard beak but at the same time the scorpion too could easily kill it if it is not very careful. Stubbornly and with his chest out like that of an unusually big crab he studied them for some time. He was a Mosotho giant. His eyes were very red like that of a goat head cooked with its horns. His lips were dry and thick and out of him barked the voice like that of a dog inside a cave:

"Oh you Satans, you are playing games. I will fix you because you do things deliberately thinking that God is great!" He turned as he spoke. He walked like an old woman who could be accused of witchcraft. He went out and banged the huge door of the jail. Later the Christian prisoners heard the clinking sound of a padlock unlocking the door. They just looked at each other. Letlotla was about to start a hymn when the door of the prison hall opened. The hymn dried into their throats and silence evaded the place. After the door opened, the warder came in accompanied by five of his men. They carried big scissors and buckets full of cold water.

Each prisoner's hair was cut as according to the order given by the warder. Hair fell to the floor like grass that is been evaded by termites. After some time, one lady came followed by one of the men and they picked and carried all they hair to the prison garbage. An order immediately came from the warder that all the water from the buckets should be poured on the floor of the prison hall. That was done. He ordered them to fetch more water and pour it on the ground until it reached about three inches. After that he locked the prison and left the believers to think. He then went to the commissioner and gave a report of all that he had ordered.

It was almost during the late afternoon and hunger had begun troubling the believers. Each one of them tried to ignore it but it kept pestering them slowly. Evangel Letlotla and Mmolaaditso were the ones who led the hymn. When their bibles and song books got confiscated at the Kgotla they managed to hide a few Sesotho song books in their pockets. And now at this point they had opened them and led the choir so that the rest of the believers could follow.

Those who entered the jail for the first time were restless, looking almost at every corner every now and then. The prison walls were very big and there was no way a person could break them and escape. It was very dark when the door was closed with a very small light entering through the two small spaces. It was very difficult to tell what time of the day it was. At the far corner of the jail there was a rusty bucket. The stench that came from that bucket could kill a person. At first some women tried to cover their noses but it didn't last long when the stench finally entered through their noses forcefully. The chanting of the songs made matters worse. Because of not taking a shower, the armpits of some believers were also singing. Their dirty teeth too worsened the situation when they sang. When all these smells mixed, it made a stench like that from a decomposed dog.

The door opened and Modiko was pushed inside the prison by the warder. He fell on the wet ground with his tummy like a pig. He joined others as water dripped from his khaki shorts. When the door was closed, the believers realized that the sun was about to set. For a short while the singing was paused and Letlotla asked Modiko to relate what they had done to him.

"Some of the servants felt sorry for me and gave me some food. The chief took his car but when he returned he came with Dr. Lovelace…" Modiko reported. One of the women interrupted.

"With who? Ramolaisi?"

"Ee, Mma. Lovelace. Ramolaisi." Modiko cleared his throat and continued:

"Ramolaisi looked very happy for they were laughing very much with the chief. He even said this in my presence; '…you should take serious steps for them khosi. They are taking our members!' He said that he told the commissioner that we should be poured with water for the whole night. That thing is not a pastor!" Modiko finished and then wept bitterly.

The rest of the believers looked at each other and wondered if there could be severe punishment other than what they already had. Already they had to stand on their feet all the time and they couldn't sit or sleep.

"Had he not come to nurse your wounds when he came?" Enquired the pastor.

"No…not at all. Actually, he never even felt sorry for me when he saw me for the first time. He kept on praising the chief and saying that the commissioner was going to deal with us and ensure that he gives more severe punishment. He also mentioned that the commissioner had invited the chief for dinner. He also stated that the commissioner was going to write other white people in England to give the chief a decorative award of O.B.E."

Modiko's wounds, just like that of other believers were swollen and sticking to the clothes. He felt the anger as if it was burning the heart out of his chest. He felt hatred piling up in his mind. It was one of a kind that rubbed him bitterly inside and out. He felt the hatred for a white man and every human being worshiping him like he was God. He threw himself into a sense of self introspection when he remembered the commandment which the pastor encouraged them with in the morning. It said you must love your enemy and pray for him.

"How did you arrive here now?" One of the women in the congregation asked

"The police brought me here and handed me to the prison warders. This is how I came here," Modiko responded.

When their hunger was getting worse, the believers comforted themselves by the sermon which says a man does not live with bread alone. Letlotla reminded them how Jesus himself spent forty days without food but depending on God's spirit alone. They sang their hymn much louder. Outside the jail, the warders prepared the hose pipes by tying them on the taps. They were five in number but the hose pipes were just three. Three of them pulled the hosepipes towards the jail whereas others carried buckets which were full of water.

Some prisoners on the other side of the jail who had begun to sing with the believers stopped when one of them who looked through the hole of the jail told them what he saw the warders doing. The prison was divided in two parts, one side was for males and the other was for female prisoners. But because there were no female prisoners, all the believers were locked on the female prison so that they don't mix with other prisoners lest they could become converts too. This was according to the advice given by Dr. Lovelace which he dictated to the commissioner during the night he had visited him. It was even forbidden for pastors from small churches to preach to the prisoners during the Lord's days. All this was according to the directions given by Dr. Lovelace.

As the hymn was still loud and strong, the door unlocked and was wide opened. It was almost getting dark when the chief warder opened the taps. A chill wind of tebatsabarwaledi season had swept all the clouds in the sky and it was clear. When the door opened the wind flew inside the jail like a fly flying into a bucket full of milk. The hymn continued as if nothing had happened. The believers started to shrink their bodies to prepare for cold water. The eyes of the warders shone from the dark like touches. They gnashed their lower lips and held the hose pipes with masculine strength. The water splashed through the pipes and the men put their dirty fingers on the hosepipes to increase pressure just as gardeners would do.

They pointed the hose pipes to the believers and as the water fell on them there was an involuntary noise coming out of their lungs. At first, they tried to block with their hands, then they used their jackets but it didn't work as the water penetrated. The wet clothes stuck to their bodies revealing the stretch marks and corners in their bodies. However, they continued singing. They chief warder tried to send water to their mouths so that they could stop singing because they would get in trouble if the doctor, the chief, and the commissioner heard their chants. The believers turned their back from the water to prevent water from entering their eyes or choking them.

After some time, probably a time that could be taken by a boy who doesn't know how to milk a cow with long tits, the chief warder ordered them to stop. He studied the believers for a while as they continued singing. He then instructed that the door should be left open so that the cold air could flow in and out as it pleases. That was done.

The directive from the commissioner was that they should be poured with water until they kept quiet since before that they disturbed his sleep all night. However, the singing continued, even though some were not able to sing because of shivering as the cold wind blew at them.

The chief warder was very patient when it came to making a prisoner under his care suffer. He was from Lesotho and came to Botswana at the invitation of the British rule to stop the problems that had erupted some years back. Batswana police men were not able to solve this problem but the Whiteman's rule brought Basotho because of their reputation of stubbornness and gigantic body. In addition, this man worked for a long time in South Africa where he dealt with dangerous criminals. Those murderers whose hair would literally grow instantly while the other side of the head is still getting shaved. These men, shedding human blood didn't mean anything to them at all. It was just like water which they could spill like a child who is playing with soil on the ground. Sand was put into their food and they could pull a garbage vehicle with their bodies every morning at the heart of the winter. Their feet would tear apart and flatten because of the cold. The prison was built using hard rocks from the foundation to the top. There was clay soil on the ground and it was mixed with water so that it looked like the kraal of pigs. The chief warder was the only one who could handle them and all the torturing was done by him. Right now, as he poured cold water on even small children, he was not at all worried.

He gave a command again and the taps were opened again. The water poured until midnight. It was now beginning to flood the foundation of the jail. All the lights which had been lit went off and silence permeated the village, except that there were barking dogs here or there. The singing of the believers was now louder than before when silence spread across the land. The hymn carried a message which said, 'Father pull me when the spear is above me.'

Chapter 7

This place was called Kgalagadi Desert by Mmamosadinyana's intellectuals and their allies. It is a place with a grass tall enough to conceal a cow that is walking in it. The bush was stuck together like dirty hair. So, the ordinary people who are not the Queen's intellectuals have always sat and wondered what a desert meant. Is it a place where drinking water is very scarce? Is the desert a place without any plants except the sand dunes which are spread like the foam of milk in a bucket? Their heads locked until they finally gave up. What is the use of giving ourselves a headache with the mysteries known only to our forefathers?

At the north-west side of Molepolole, about six days of walking there is a place where Bakwena and Bangwato reside. This intersection is called Lephepe. The chief of this village was by the fire place in the evening when one of his men came sweating. He appeared as if he came from a very far place.

"My master, I'm here to inform you about the unusual story from the liars in your village," the man said after he greeted.

"Why don't you unveil the liars with their lies so we can see their nakedness? Lies never last, they are short footed. Once you say it will show, the lies will coil themselves like a millipede, and they will show shyness like a man who sees his in-laws," the chief proclaimed. His eyes were fixed on the men as if he would tear him apart to see his inner self.

"When I was looking for my lost donkey, I passed by this boy called Tshokele, I mean Kenalemang's son. He told me that tomorrow morning, when the buttocks of children are still warm, the prophets of Motlha-o-Etla will be baptizing their followers in the stream where we drink water," he spit the mucus and it coiled itself with the dust.

"What are you saying monna? In the water that we drink? What do they want to see? A donkey giving birth daylight or a rat having grown horns?" The chief said as he gnashed his teeth with anger and stood up.

****

The sun of that morning of June rose at the top of dark trees. It was red in color like the eye of a drunkard. The birds sang their melodies in praise of the creator of the day. The main stream of Lephepe was filled with water. The reason was that rains had continued through the end of July.

By the time the men from Lephepe village arrived carrying axes, machetes, and spears on their shoulders, they found Evangel Bamosotla on the fifth baptismal candidate. They engulfed the stream and shouted to the believers to come out of the water, otherwise they threatened to chop them. The baptism stopped and the evangel went out of the water. Those who helped him to hold and pass to him the baptismal candidates also went out of the water. The flock was surrounded by the village men.

This evangel was called Bamosotla because he liked to preach about how the Jews persecuted Jesus. He viewed anyone who persecuted children of God as a Jew and as such any believer who did loving deeds of Jesus was supposed to be persecuted by Jews who did not have faith. That is why when he immediately came out of the water, while water was still dripping from his clothes he said:

"My fellow brothers, do not be amazed at this. This is exactly what was foretold by the Lord when he said: 'If a living tree is dying, then a dead one is trouble. Weep not for I, but for yourselves. Because they persecuted him, we should also expect affliction...'"

A man who appeared like the leader of mophato opened his red mouth. His teeth were black and stuck together like an old donkey. His eyes were red and smaller like those of a cat that gets irritated by a beam of the light. He said:

"Let us go to the chief. You swim on clean water like pigs, come on!" He said as he lifted the wooden body of the peak he was carrying.

When the believers tried to go Bamosotla stopped them. "Hang on there men of God! Just wait." He turned and faced men from mophato. "Sirs, let us talk first so that tomorrow you won't say I never

64

warned you that the Egyptian plaques are falling upon you," he said as he gestured with his hands to tell people to sit down.

The leader, whose name was Kgwengweng, thought this was very despising more specially when he saw the rest of the congregation sitting down as well as most of his men. He got furious and talked in his language. He said to his men:

"Metshe he doge. Dogang! Tshuma nta le lekgantsetse. Ba butse kga ritshobane tsenu. Ba rwanyeng bo modolakga." He said in his anger suggesting that the believers should be beaten.

However, the men did not touch anyone. Some members of the church were their relatives, except Bamosotla who came from Molepolole. He had been sent by the elders to reenergize the flock in Lephepe. And some of these men were members of Dr. Lovelace's church, they had been taught that it is a sin to kill another human being. They were very familiar with the ten plagues that the Lord nearly used to finish the family in Egypt. So, when evangel Bamosotla alluded to the ten plagues they knew very well what he was talking about. Who on earth could stand the event, whereby useful and scarce water such as that in Lephepe river gets turned into blood?

One of the men from this group heard the command of their leader, Kgwengweng. He came with his machete raised on the air and struck one woman who was carrying the baby on her back. Three of the men held him and his machete fell to the ground.

"Don't kill the woman and baby! A few days back he defecated on his clothes because he was scared of the leopard," one of the men mocked.

When some of the men broke into laughter, Evangel Letlotla started to speak when he realized the Kgwengweng was determined. He then said:

"Men of the chief, let us finish first this holy work and after that we will come with you to the chief. Otherwise you are just inviting problems for yourselves for the Lord will face you directly with his plagues."

"This God of your church likes to stumble people? Why are you starting with us on our river? You are washing your dirt from the very place we drink water from," Kgwengweng asked with his eyes wide open.

"It is not our intent to provoke anyone. It is a command from Jesus Christ himself. He opened the scripture and read for the men."

One of the men shouted from the back and asked a question thus expressing his feelings. His lips were just like that of a toad. Evangel Bamosotla realized almost immediately what caused his lips to be like that. When he opened his mouth, he could only see his tongue licking the red and toothless gums. He held one of his nose holes and blocked it using his figure. He blew the dark mucus through the other side of the nose and said:

"Why can't your church baptize inside the house like Ramolaisi's church? And also, why don't you dig a pit which you can use for this very purpose? Right now, some of you here had gone to the bushes and did not wipe themselves well. I like Ramolaisi's church for the fact that it doesn't cause anyone to consume dirt. The reason why the church of a Whiteman is better than that of a Motswana is that a Whiteman knows a lot about hygiene."

Evangel Letlotla looked at him and he was so determined to answer him carefully and eloquently. He then asked:

"Do you have a document that shows that you are a member of Dr. Lovelace's church?"

"No."

"Well now you are just like someone who hates it. You are not its member just like you are not the member of this church. You are in a way also fighting it. You don't like it and you don't have anything to prove you do. You are just praising it with your lips and that is hypocrisy. Now answering your other question, the Lord's command is that baptism should be performed in a natural river, not in a man-made artificial dam. Even Jesus Christ himself was baptized in Jordan, a natural river. It was a river where people drank from just like this one. It is not done for the first time. Baptism, according to the way God commanded in Palestine it was done in rivers where people drank from. You are actually sinning against God to stop us from doing his will. Baptizing inside the house is just founded on personal feeling rra!"

Kgwengweng didn't know much about the bible—actually he couldn't even read. At times he would just look at the pictures when he picked a paper that had been used to wrap a package. When he looked at the alphabets he just saw tails and scorpions only—the drawings of centipedes. But there was only one account that he knew from the bible, it was the account of King Herod. He knew that this king died a very painful death when we got eaten alive by maggots. The reason was because he was fighting against Jesus, the same man that Bamosotla has just talked about.

Kgwengweng found himself fearing that this fate might befall him as well. He therefore softened his heart and wanted the believers to be killed by something else, but at the same time- not him. An account which had become a conundrum in the village was a question of who the real killer was between the hangman and the judge was who gives someone a death sentence. Language itself could not debate this complex question. Some people would say it was the judge, some would say it is the one who operates the instrument used to behead a prisoner. Now Kgwengweng wanted to be like a judge who gives a death sentence while he is not guilty himself. Pontius Pilate too washed his hands after sentencing someone to death. At least for him he was saved from being eaten alive by maggots.

It was known that a great dragon lived inside Lephepe river. On the side where this dragon lived no man or cow could go. Recently Tladinyana's cow went there. It was last seen standing there, as if it was engrossed at seeing something very interesting, but it disappeared for good at the same spot. Because of this, Kgwengweng requested that if Bamosotla wished to continue with baptism he should not do it on the side where people drink. He pointed where the great dragon stayed as the side where they could perform their baptism. Bamosotla thanked Kgwengweng and glimpsed at the congregation. Before he could even say anything two of the men from mophato told him that a big snake lives there. They talked about the cows and donkeys which have been devoured by this dragon. They also related to him about a young boy who once drowned and his body was never seen until this day. Those who were going to get baptized confirmed that story. The evangel looked at them the way a person who is so full would look at the expiring meal.

"For those who want to see salvation, and be freed from Egypt, let them follow me," he said as he paced towards that direction.

Women who had come to fetch some water at the river stood there watching, and therefore the group looking at this had increased. The evangel entered into the water until it reached somewhere near his breast. After the prayed, baptism resumed and young men brought the baptismal candidates. Since only five people were left to get baptized they finished after some time. Kgwengweng was left speechless when he saw that nothing that he expected happened. Now at the end of the service, the evangel went to him and said:

"The work of the Lord is now over so it is up to you to take us wherever you want."

Kgwengweng removed his tattered hat and pleaded the evangel to lead the congregation to the chief's place. Evangel Bamosotla led the congregation with a very loud hymn. All the men from the regime followed, and they carried axes, spears and machetes on their hands like a farmer who is coming back from the field in the afternoon. The chief had just finished drinking his beer by the time they arrived. He put his container beside him and then pulled the hat to his eyes so that he could look like a vicious lion.

Chapter 8

Modiko got awakened from his sleep by the noisy footsteps of the nurse on duty. She was covered with a loin cloth that stuck on her thin waist as she came through the security door. His heart climbed all the way up to the throat and blocked it. It was unbearably painful when he swallowed the saliva. She put her tray next to the bed where a boy who sat next to Modiko lay.

"Open your mouth!" The nurse shouted. The little boy tried to open his mouth but because of his poor health he did things very slowly in a lethargic way.

"I said open your mouth. Are you deaf, or are trying to perform for me? If you break this thermometer with these corn grains you call teeth you will be in trouble." She slapped the boy on his face after which she placed the thermometer on the boy's mouth. A tear dropped from the boy's face but he didn't say anything. After a while she pulled out the thermometer from the boy's mouth and then used a cotton wool to wipe it. She shook it before studying it. The mercury went down a little bit. When she noticed it, she went back to the boy and used her figures to open his mouth the way a person would do to a baby goat. She took it out again and wiped it and then recorded the findings on the paper that hung at the back of the bed. She held the boy's hand as she kept noting time. She scribbled something on a piece of paper.

After she administered a pill to the boy, she used an injection to such a whitish medicine. She placed another needle on the injection. She injected the boy on the buttocks until the boy responded. When she removed the ejection, blood came out and she took a cotton wool, and then instructed the boy to hold it until the blood stopped.

"Hold on to that carefully and stop playing. You think you will ever be a kid again?" The nurse yelled as she pushed the boy's hand into his buttocks.

All this while, Modiko watched this incident with fear and anger. He swore he would never ever in his life get married to a nurse. The nurse pushed a trolley towards him. He felt sorry for himself and held his breath for a while. The nurse's face shone with some blood which showed she had been obviously burned by excessive use of makeup. By looking at her legs it was easy to tell that she was a black person, darker in complexion. Her neck and hands also told the same story about her color. After she studied the paper that hang at the back of the bed she turned to Modiko.

"Are you the one coming from jail?" She asked loudly so that other patients could hear her question.

"Yes madam, it's me." Modiko answered shyly. Some patients raised their heads from their sickbeds.

"Let me see the wounds." She pulled the blankets from Modiko although they had stuck to his wounds. When the red wounds pilled off he felt the pain piercing through his heart. But he quietly endured the pain for he feared getting slapped. For the second time the nurse asked loudly so that other patients could hear.

"If you have started going to jail at this age what will you be when you are a grown up? What had you done?"

"I was found worshiping at the church that the chief doesn't want."

"Are you a member of Zion Christian Church?"

"No, I go to Motlha-o-Etla."

"Is it not like the Zion church? Do they clap their hands?" The nurse asked.

"No, they are not the same. At Motlha-o-Etla we don't clap our hands, we don't dance or play drums. The only thing that we do in the same way is baptism because we baptize in the river and not in the house." Modiko started coughing bitterly.

The nurse now changed from her behavior, becoming polite for some time. She felt sorry to see such a small boy slashed and torn like that although he was innocent. She thought of how she was forced to be a member of Dr. Lovelace's church. Since she came from Motshodi, she used to go to Dutch Reform church but after she did standard six she came to look for a job at Dr. Lovelace's hospital. Dr. Lovelace told her that she could get a job only if she quit her church and joined his church. As a result, she was forced to quit the church that she liked because she needed a job to keep surviving. She felt very sorry when she heard Modiko coughing that she said:

"The reason for this cough is because of exposure to water and cold. Has the rain caught you at the bush during winter lately?"

Modiko related how they spent two nights in the jail and how water was poured on them every night to silence them.

They were talking in a low voice such that other patients were now surprised how the nurse was now very nice to him all of a sudden. She gave him three pills and an injection and continued with her questions about what happened at the jail. She could have continued but not until she got interrupted by the senior nurse who had been looking at her al this while. Her anger was not genuine, it was one of a kind that could be called a showy display mixed with pride.

"When do you think you will attend other patients if you stay on this child for so long? Are you people trying to get married? Don't you know that the prayer is about to start? Oh people! How can someone just relax on just one patient?" She was left embarrassed for being reprimanded in front of the patients. The senior nurse went back to her seat shout and making a lot of noise with the rubbing of her thighs.

When things went to normal, Modiko felt the pain on his lungs. It was like fire had been set right on his lungs. He felt weak that he doubted if he would ever recuperate. He thought that he was going to die. When he thought about death he got very scared. He stopped thinking about such things and remembered how he got admitted at the hospital.

That morning, his father, Evangel Letlotla came carrying him on his bicycle. It was just right after the morning prayer. He went on when it was his turn. He found Dr. Lovelace on his consultation room with his medical instruments stuck on his ears.

"What is the problem mosumane?" He asked with a very strong accent.

"I cough a lot and I have chest pains and a running nose."

"When did you start to get sick?"

"Since Tuesday morning." Modiko replied after using his fingers to count.

"Do you wear enough clothes at night?"

"Yes sir, I do. I wear three blankets."

"The cause of your illness is due to exposure to too much cold and water. Have you lately been exposed to the cold?" The doctor asked as he played with his stethoscope.

Modiko told him about the night he spent at the Kgotla without warm clothing. And he also related to him about how cold water was poured on them for two days during the night at jail. His face immediately changed like that of someone who is saddened by what he heard.

"Oh my child, are you a member of Motlha-o-Etla church?"

"Yes doctor." He replied.

"The love of God has not yet settled on earth. People are persecuting others. A time will come when people will know the glory of God and peace will abide on earth. Persecutions and afflictions will come to an end. Why don't you join my church so that you can avoid persecutions? In my church there are no such things."

"I will see after I've healed, doctor."

"Do you go to school?" he asked.

"Yes doctor."

"What level are you doing?"

"I am done with standard six. Right now, I am doing standard seven at Kgari Sechele." Modiko responded, but he was impatient because he wanted to be attended.

"You are such an educated person. You shouldn't clap hands and keep dancing to Satan's songs. Just come to my church and I will send you to a pastoral school and give you good medicine." The doctor didn't wait for the response but he continued with his work.

"What is your name?"

"I'm Modiko Letlotla."

"How old are you?"

"I'm sixteen years old."

The doctor scribbled all that he said. He then spoke to him in English:

"You have pneumonia. It was caused by exposure to the cold for a long time and the cold water that was poured on you. You will be admitted for about a week in the hospital. Well, but if you show signs of improvement you will be released. Will you be able to walk by yourself to the patient beds?"

"Yes doctor, I will try."

Modiko tried to stand up but he was shaking like an egg yolk that was not well done. He fell to the floor on his buttocks. Madalambijana was called to carry him in a wheelchair. When he arrived at the patient room he noticed that all nurses starred at him as if they were looking at a rotten fish.

They removed his khaki shirt which had been hardened by water and dirt. The shirt pilled off some of his flesh from the wounds caused by Senwamoro's cane. They took him to the bathtub where they washed him like a huge pig. They asked him if he was from the cattle post and when last he did take a shower. Some even asked if he has ever taken a shower ever since he was born. After they bathed him they applied a very itchy medicine to the wounds. The pain it caused could cause someone to wet their pants.

Modiko came back from whatever he was thinking of. He held his waist and he felt way better compared to the pain he felt before. The pills even reduced the burning in his lungs that he felt earlier. When he raised his eyes, he found that a short man who distributes meals to the patients had brought his soft porridge and put it by his bed. It was maize meal with reddish corn and a very thin slice of bread. The tea he had brought could make you throw out by just looking at it. Modiko thought of Tau, the old man. He called this kind of tea 'urine from donkeys'. The porridge that was served too was poorly done and looked as if it had been pasted on the plate. He just forced himself to eat that garbage but later realized that he just worsened his hunger. It could have been better if he hadn't eaten anything at all. He wished he could call that man but fear and shyness could not allow him.

As Evangel Letlotla was just about to leave he saw Rre Tlholego entering through the main gate. He was forced to entertain him and show some respect based on the words which say you must respect your father and mother. His father had died a few years back and two years after that his mother passed on too, just after the village relocated from the hilly area. Just before her demise, the old woman told them that the ancestors and her forefathers were calling her. She talked about a new religion, which Mokganedi had joined (or Jeremia Letlotla for he changed to this apostolic name after he got baptized). In short, this is what the old woman said:

"Mokganedi my child, I am going to my forefathers at the land of my ancestors. And I am going to the place where all the earthly burdens that I am carrying on my shoulders will be removed. I will have rest and stay like a queen and will not be slaving for anyone. At that place, there is no a king or a servant, a Mosarwa or Mokwena. This is the place where we are all equal."

The old woman was looking at the side of the hill as if she was staring at something very interesting. Her voice changed instantly and she talked like an earthly person. She became a mother who was advising her child.

"This new religion of people who come and then go is strange to us. It could be good but at the same time it could be like a python that catches a duiker by changing its colors and using the delicacy of its eyes. Do not forget your traditions because of this new religion. It is ignorance and short lived happiness to take pleasure in a strange religion after you have forsaken your ancestors, your forefathers. It will give you the type of joy which will humiliate you by the time you wake up." The old woman lay her head on the pillow and slept everlastingly. Although Letlotla did not agree with what his mother said, these words touched him. He dropped a tear. Rre Tlholego was there when all these things happened.

"And God told Abraham: Stand up and Go. Leave behind your people on this land and in your father's house. Go to the land that I will show you..." Letlotla recalled this verse in his mind. He imagined himself as Abraham who left a family that did not have faith. Their hearts were controlled by the devil himself.

It had been about fourteen years since the death of his mother. The Evangel thought it wise to honor the words of his late mother by adopting Rre Tlholego as his father so that his days may be lengthened. But all this time his heart refused for he thought that spiritual people did not have anything to do with the worldly people. Under no circumstances could frost and fire co-exist. A cat and a rat will always be enemies forever. How can wickedness and just live together? How can a sinner and a child of God stay together? That is not possible regardless of whether they are relatives or not. He thought for a minute that his body was like a kraal with two bulls which fight ceaselessly. One of the bulls wanted to have all the power.

"Koti!Koti!" Rre Tlholego knocked.

"Come in, rraetsho." The evangel answered as he prepared the chair for his uncle to sit on. They greeted one another. The old man gave the details about his health and family, his journeys on the village and all the things he saw, both good and bad. He mentioned that the ancestors had remembered them because it was warm that day. The fact that Letlotla had been released from prison was a testimony that the ancestors were there for him. After he talked at length about these things, he asked:

"How are you yourself?"

"We are fine rra, just as you find us. Modiko is the one who is not well. I intend to go and check him in the afternoon. His mother came yesterday from the lands. She went to her mother's house. One of her cousin's daughters had a miscarriage," he said.

"Now where are you going? You are wearing a nice suit." Rre Tlholego inquired.

"Am I dressed up? These are night clothes. They are not formal clothes."

"Well what we know is that you have to take off your clothes and get naked when you go to bed. You young people dress up?" The evangel laughed. Rre Tlholego asked if the evangel wanted to pass

75

through the village with his night clothes since he appeared to be on the way when he came.

"No, I was not going anywhere. I was just on my way to the toilet."

"You don't go to the bush like everybody? We don't want excretion on our compound. We throw it away at the hill over there." The evangel laughed, this time for a longer time. After that he asked Rre Tlholego if they didn't use night clothes when he went to fight at the war.

"There was no time to get dressed up for the night. You think we had gone for a wedding there? We slept with rifles on our side. The minute you close your eyes you would think about the Germans bringing destruction to the soil that you are stepping on."

The evangel asked his uncle if he should make him some tea.

"No, don't bother yourself my elder brother's child. I just took a cup of tea at home before I came here."

After all the humor had finished, Rre Tlholego almost instantly assumed a very serious face. He stretched fingers in all of his limbs before he glanced at the sky. It was clear, not even a small cloud showed and the wind too was no more. It was warm. He also looked at Letlotla's house; it was a combination of a traditional hut and a modern house. From the foundation it was built with soil but at the top it had bricks and cement. It also had pillars and its roofing was made of corrugated iron. He knew the inside of the house very well. Pictures of angels and unbelievers being pulled into the fiery fire by Satan hung from the wall. Nonsense! He thought to himself. Rre Tlholego believed that Satan is poverty. Anything other than that there it is not Satan. After he looked at the surrounding like that, he looked at Letlotla in the eyes:

"I just wanted to find out how you are doing and how the judgment went."

"Yes sir, that's very good news to hear." The evangel stood up from his seat and blew the fire which had begun to die as the sun rose.

"The chief's men gave us a hard time. They had said that we were going to stay for five months in jail. We were surprised that after two days we were released at the chief's order. We only spent a Monday night and a Tuesday night. On Wednesday we were told that we would be let free. One of the boys who chops firewood for the commissioner told us that the commissioner had instructed the chief to release us. He continued to relate that we disturbed the commissioner's sleep at night when we sang and praised God with hymns. Our hymn could force a pig out of its den.

Inside the jail we spent the whole night standing on our feet. They poured water on us because they wanted us to keep quiet. Because of that cold water, a lot of children caught flu just as Modiko caught pneumonia. Our teeth gnashed throughout the night. On Wednesday morning we were led to the kgotla. There he told us how he had the all the power to take us back to jail again. He fined each one of us thirteen cows. We told him that we were not going to pay anything. We are determined to suffer just like our lord did. The chief and his henchmen are spoiled from all the fines they have been taking from us to feed their bellies. This time we told him that a cane has only killed a rat, he can beat us the way he wants but our reward is in the heaven. If mankind's souls are united they can stand the most severe affliction and persecution. Well, he kept saying that we should give him those cows."

His eyes shone as he spoke. He patted the chair to put emphasis to his reasons. Rre Tlholego paid attention all this time. His rested his beard covered chin on his knees. When he learnt that his brother's son had finished he asked another question.

"Exactly what is your goal about this? Is it because you want to just despise your chieftaincy with a Whiteman's religion and God who comes from these papers you call the bible?"

"No uncle, we are not in any way despising our chieftaincy system or Setswana way. Is worshiping God destructive or unlawful? The chief himself is a convert of Dr. Lovelace's church. Now he just wants to stop us from worshiping because a white man tells him that we are taking members of his church. That is why he is persecuting us. We are not killing anyone, we are not using witchcraft, we don't steal. Where exactly do we break the law rangwane?"

"Okay, there I understand you. But I think you are all derailed. You, the chief and the people like you, you are all just idling in the bush. You have left your tradition to worship a whiteman's God. You are just like bats, which up to now we don't know whether they are birds or rats. As for you, we don't even know if you are Batswana or Makgowa. You have left the ancestors of your forefathers and followed other people's ancestors. Do you know the story of a jackal?"

At this point, the evangel had had enough, he was irritated and anger burned him from inside. He however just controlled his temper so that he could preach for this sinner sitting next to him. His primary goal is to bring those who walk in the dark into the flock of the lord. After some time, he said:

"No, I don't know that story rra"

"Once upon a time a jackal smelled delicious meat in front of him. It was the smell of chicken meat and that of pork. They were right next to each other. Because of greediness, jackal wanted to go and eat all the food. How so? As he went there he could sense that the smell came from two opposite directions. He kept on trying to go after each of these two smells until he finally got torn apart. He died before he could even eat any of that meat."

"So, what I see is that you converts of this new religion, you are trying to be Whites and Batswana at the same time."

The old man kept quiet for some time. He gazed at the evangel's house for some time and tried to recall the name that Bakwena had adopted to call this house. They named it a mule, a baby of a horse and a donkey, hence it cannot be a modern house or a traditional Setswana hut.

Chapter 9

Modiko felt that he was making some progress in his recuperation. And, almost all of his wounds having healed, he was not feeling the pain anymore. The scorching pain in his lungs had quieted like a whirlwind that had just passed. Because his mother was at home most of the time, he was not hungry as she would often carry some food for him to eat while at the hospital.

Two other children were brought to the hospital and were admitted into a room next to his—these two poor kids were with him when cold water was poured on their bodies using a hose. They were brought to the same hospital just two days after he was admitted. They both had died and this frightened Modiko very much, for he thought that he too was going to die. However, as time passed he had some hope.

If there is one thing that really shocked him it is that he was still scared of death although he had been baptized. He knew very well that when he dies he was going straight to heaven. His pastor, Mmolaaditso, had preached that death is only to be feared by the sinners because they also feared dying a second death in the future. But as for him, why was he so scared? He was introspective, but he never found an answer.

Wednesday of the following week he was released from the hospital. He felt fully recovered and energetic, like a lamb, after spending a full week in the hospital. During that morning, the evangelist was there and he paid all the money that was required. He then rode with Modiko in his bicycle to go home. Upon arriving, the children in that yard were very happy to see Modiko. Some of them were even inspecting him from toe to head and asked how it felt to sleep on the bed that belonged to the whites.

Was he eating the same food that white people ate? The kids wondered. There were many questions that he was asked including how he dealt with the slaps and painful injections from the nurses at the hospital.

His grandfather Rre Tlholego was also present.

"My grandson how are you feeling now?" He asked while shoving a pipe into his mouth.

"*Ee Rra* I am fine." Modiko responded.

"After you finish eating you must come over to my place. I want you to go buy me some meat at Segataborokwe's place over there."

After he finished eating Modiko did go to his grandfather's place. His mother had bought him a new nice shirt and a pair of trousers. He dressed and ran to Rre Tlholego's house. After he greeted Rre Tlholego's family, he said to him:

"Son, why don't we go together to that hill over there this upcoming Saturday? I want to go and look for something there."

Modiko agreed at once. There was a special connection between these two, sort of a special bond that exists between a grandpa and his grandson. Rre Tlholego wished to see Modiko taking the leadership of the Dikoloi clan. Modiko's father, Jeremiah, had refused to lead that *kgotla* after his father died. When his people wanted to appoint him a *Kgosana* he refused, claiming that the kingdoms of this earth will rot. He said he wanted to make his own kingdom in the heaven where nothing can defy his rule. Hence, all this time Rre Tlholego was just hoping that Modiko would assume the leadership of this clan when he gets older. The old man wanted to mentor him by himself so that he becomes a firm leader.

However, there was one thing that troubled him about this child—Modiko was already a baptized member. He was worried that he might copy that bad influence from his father. Just recently Modiko spoke to the chief's brother the way he liked and this was exactly the stubbornness he copied from this father. But he was doing that because he was still a child. If this boy can talk back the way he liked to the most feared chief, whom men stutter and wet their pants when they must address, that means he could face the Whiteman and say with obstinacy: "No! I will not kiss your ass!" In Setswana tradition, they say a child is a rod and it was better that he adjusts his grandson's attitude while he was still young. At least he could do that and show him into the right path of tradition before he hardens. Therefore, it was his intention to try him the same way an ant tests the warmth of an ash heap before they pass through it.

As for Modiko, he liked the old man for his ability to tell endless stories. He told many stories, and every time he managed to keep their newness and freshness. He would often tell him stories about the war between the British and the Germans, military tanks, and rifles. It was unlike his father, who could only talk about the bible and the stories in it. At first, he found some of these stories quite interesting, and then eventually they made him feel uncomfortable and scared. He did not find hearing stories of people getting burnt in a fire by another human being-like creature very interesting.

Modiko enjoyed his grandfather's explanations especially every time when he tried to share with Rre Tlholego some of the things that he was taught at school. One day he once made a fool of himself when he tried to convince his grandfather that that the earth was round in shape.

"You know if you drank alcohol I would think that you are probably drunk. The earth is round! I am beginning to suspect that you secretly drink alcohol my boy." Rre Tlholego responded in a very casual tone. Modiko then said, "But grandfather I am telling you the truth. The earth is round just like an orange or melon."

"At least if you said it is round and flat like a phonograph record I could understand. I thought you are learning something worthwhile at school but I can now see that you are not learning anything at all. Why then are we not falling? These cattle you see here would be falling on us if that was the case."

"But grandfather they told us that the earth is round, and it is also constantly rotating…"

Pointing to the house at the back of the yard, Rre Tlholego interjected, "*Monna wee!* Bring a melon from that house." Modiko brought the melon. It was very big and enough to stretch a boy's waist. The old man further instructed him to bring some corn grains. After doing all this, he stuffed his pipe with some tobacco. He used his finger to pick a glowing coal and stacked it into the pipe. He used all his energy to inhale it, leaving the bones in his cheeks exposed.

"Okay young man, let's say this melon is the earth, according to the way you the educated think or understand it." He stuffed the pipe into his mouth and sent to the air about five clouds of smoke which smelled like wet chicken droppings. Modiko choked. Rre Tlholego held the pipe using his hand and then continued.

"Let's pretend these corn grains are humans, horses, donkeys, elephants and everything living on earth. Place those grains on top of the 'earth' then." Carefully, Modiko tried to put the maize on top of the melon, but despite doing that delicately some of the grains kept falling off to the ground. When he looked at his grandfather he found him long gone, laughing his teeth out. His blackened teeth were left exposed. After a while, Modiko finally finished putting all the grains on top of the melon. Rre Tlholego looked at it for a while before he issued another command: "Now young man, your people live at the top only? There are no inhabitants underneath?"

"Some people live there; the problem is that the maize grains keep on falling. But…"

"But what? What does this teach you? How can humans live on a round earth? You had earlier mentioned that the same earth is constantly rotating. Rotate it then! Do that and see what will happen to the maize grains."

When Modiko touched the melon, all the grains of maize fell off to the ground at once. That was the funniest thing that Rre Tlholego saw for that day, for when all this happened he could not stop laughing. "Young man, I'm already very sick so please don't finish me off by making me laugh this much. Let me go and see Mokgaodi, I have been thinking that you receive proper education at school but I just realized that what you are being taught is nothing but stools of chicken and pigs. Hi-Hi-Hiii!" As he talked he shoved his pipe into one of the pockets of his coat.

Rre Tlholego gave Modiko two shillings so he could go and buy him some meat from Segataborokgwe's shop. Meat from his shop was cheaper but plenty. It was way much better than buying from Tlhakodimajwe's place. Modikwe left to buy meat for his grandfather. When he arrived, people stared at him and some of them paved way for him as if they were scared of him. He knew very well that the reason why they behaved like this was because of his recent imprisonment. That was very clear.

Segatabokgwe was the one selling. This was not his real name but a nickname given to him by the villagers when he arrived in this country from India. By then he is said to have been poverty stricken but was eventually rescued from his poverty by a Jewish man called Tlhakodimajwe. Tlhakodimajwe hired him at his abattoir as a meat seller. At the time, Segataborokgwe wore oversized trousers and an un-ironed shirt. Due to his short height, he also continually stepped on his trousers. Stories were told that when excited, he would first of all have to jump in order to pull the pants to the level of his waist and then tie it. The same story goes without saying that he was given these trousers by Tlhakodimajwe, who was a very tall man.

After about six months Segataborokgwe was relieved. He started buying his own goats and sheep. He then hired a herd boy to look after his livestock and at the end of the year he had opened his own business. Now he looks like a big-bellied boss who scratches his belly like a rich man. But because he is very short, he cannot find the right size for his pants—therefore he is still stepping on his trousers even to this day. When he saw Modiko, he said using a heavy Indian accent of Setswana:

"*Tumela Mosimane*…How is your father *monna*? Greet him for me."

After Modiko dropped the meat at his grandfather's house he went to his house. There he found his mother and father waiting. Just when his mother was happy to see him, Modiko realized that his father was clearly agitated by something. His face looked extremely dull and cracked like clay. He was fuming.

"Where have you been?"

"I had gone to buy grandfather some meat."

"Where?"

"At Segataborokgwe's place *Rra*."

"Did they give you something to eat at your grandfather's house?"

Modiko remembered almost immediately that they were not allowed to eat food houses of sinners. "No. After dropping off the meat I came back home right away."

83

"Did you say meat? Where did you buy it?"

"At Segataborokgwe's place-"

Modiko responded knowing very well why his father wanted to know where he bought the meat from. Everyone knew about Tlhakodimajwe's sinful habits. Further, he sold pork. And because of this, the evangelist had instructed all his children that they should never buy meat from his place. Tlhakodimajwe was every now and then heard openly saying that black people were remnants of Cain who murdered his brother and was sent on exile and thrown into the wilderness. Because of walking through the deserts with unbearable scorching heat, Cain's skin blackened and therefore all his offspring became black people.

Not so long about the past three months he stumbled into the evangelist. Evangelist Letlotla had just arrived from shepherding his congregation in Lentsweletau. He had spent time there preaching and redeeming the lost souls and therefore he could not speak properly, his voice was affected. He stopped by Tlhakodimajwe's shop. As usual, Tlhakodimajwe had a bottle of alcohol by his side and his belly protruded into the open air like that of a corn cricket. After he was sold the meat portion that he wanted, Tlhakodimajwe asked evangelist Letlotla where he was coming from. This two didn't know each other that much. They had never even talked about religion.

"I'm from Lentsweletau over there. I went to preach the word there." The evangelist responded.

"Whose word?" Asked the Jewish man.

"The word of God and Jesus Christ"

Evangelist Letlotla gave an honest answer without knowing the intentions of his interlocutor. He was shocked to see Tlhakodimajwe breaking down with laughter, almost spitting through the corners of his lips.

"Did you say you are from preaching the word of Jesus? Ha-Ha-Ha!" he asked with his eyes filled with tears because of laughter. He only stopped laughing when he realized that the evangelist was getting very impatient with him. He then wiped off his tears and saliva. He returned to his chair and sipped his beer and then said: "At least you should have said that you are from preaching the word of God, and not that of Jesus. So, when you pray do you pray to Jesus as well?"

Because he was very hungry, Letlotla was getting very impatient but still he was eager to know why Tlhakodimajwe was asking. When a cow whisks its tail, dung is surely on its way. He reluctantly answered him and said: "Yes, we also pray to Jesus. We pray to God the Father, the Son, and the Holy Spirit."

All the laughter erupted from his big belly. He couldn't stop and his face had shrunk from this deep laughter. After he finished laughing, and having wiped off his sweat and tears he looked at the evangelist like an elephant that would look at an ant that has just claimed could defeat an elephant. He then told the evangelist what he thought, almost offloading what had accumulated in his chest. "*Monna* it would have made sense if you worshipped God only. Not Jesus as you say." He sipped his drink and then continued: "The reason for this is simple, very simple actually—God is for us all. Moreover, he knows all languages including those spoken by Cain's offspring. As for Jesus that's a no. Jesus is a Jew, like myself. He doesn't know Setswana. He is my sister's son, Mary, and that makes him my nephew. So, if I, his uncle, pray to him he listens. When a Motswana tries to open a shop, the next day it closes. When he buys a modern car, the following day chickens lay their eggs in it. Do you know why this happens? Jesus does not listen when they pray. He is not at all related to black people. Have you ever worked at one of those South African mines?"

"Yes, I have worked there for a while." The evangelist responded

"…And how much did you earn?"

"Two shillings per day"

"You see, that's exactly what I am talking about. Myself, I made ten shillings per hour. At the end of the day I earned pounds excluding the overtime money. So *monnamogolo* you are really wasting your time because Jesus does not listen to your prayers. He doesn't!" He sipped his drink again while laughing, eyes closed. His employee too joined, just to keep his job though. That's when the evangelist left at once.

When he arrived home, he found Modiko and his younger siblings John and Petrus playing *morabaraba* with other children from the village. His wife was sitting and resting under the shadow near the wall of their house. The evangelist chased all the other children and started whipping Modiko very hard and as Modiko cried he took the small ones to their mother.

"You are busy sleeping and my children are playing Satan's games *hee?*"

Waking up from her slumber their mother responded,

"What is the problem now?"

"I found them playing *morabaraba* here but I made it very clear that such things like *morabaraba*, cards, folktales—should not be practiced in my home. I want them to grow up knowing and reading about Jesus and you just let them do as they please when I am gone."

"I didn't see them. I was way too tired and then fell asleep."

During that evening, the evangelist read for his children stories from the bible and then taught them how to sing hymns. As for the folktales and other traditional songs he did not permit them to learn. Modiko and his siblings as a result lived in constant fear, with their souls almost caged. They feared doing anything evil because of the scary stories they heard about Satan.

Chapter 10

Many days had passed and the congregation had been worshipping freely without any interference from the chief. It seemed as if a mighty whirlwind had halted and things were now back to normal. For the first time, congregants worshipped freely from the top of the hills without any intrusion from the chief's men who wanted to persecute them. They had now gotten used to this amount of persecution and it was a bit unusual that it had just stopped almost immediately and without prior warning.

Persecution is unlike bereavement, one gets used to it. A donkey can attest to this fact. Because of the amount of persecution it gets subjected to, it eventually gets used to that to a point that sometimes it won't even move, regardless of how much you whip it. The heart of the person who is subjected to persecution is like the skin of a donkey: affliction hardens it until the enemy finally gives up.

September arrived, and still no men from the regiment had come after them. They had chosen to worship at the hill to avoid unnecessary confrontation. The rain clouds had gathered, when the first rain, *sephai*, started falling. All the dry land was now transformed into a beautiful green vegetation. The hill too boasted with a green terrain. The fountains and streams likewise beamed with new life as if nature was reawakening from a deep slumber.

As for the rest of the sky which was often brownish because of winter, it cleared and looked beautifully blue like water from the big rivers. The acacia and lengana trees too boasted green hues and nice white flowers with a delicious scent. In the morning, it was easy to hear the coy scream of the donkeys beyond the river and land; something they would repeat when the night fall arrived. As for the goats, they were spread and scattered across the green patches of the land. From the deepness of the hill, baboons and pigeons dominated with their grave voices. The plants and the grass were all decorated, everything sorted according to its species. Even the red stones that lay in the spread patches had turned dark brown, as if they were soaked in water. Peace spread across the earth and nothing seemed to enter in its way.

Beneath a huge mhawa tree, with a canopy and white stem, the worshipers listened attentively as evangelist Bamosotla related to them about his trip to Lephephe. "God's work is going very well in Lephephe. When I got there, I found the flock about to lose hope. It seems Satan had already entered them. *Khadi* and beer had become a norm, and people there lived by bread and not by the Lord's spirit." He also continued to report how they were attacked by the regiment sent by the chief. He narrated everything that happened and explained that they were finally sent to the chief to await a trial.

"When we left the river, we sang very loudly that someone as far as Tshwaanyane could hear us. We called unto the Lord to reveal himself to the sinners that he was mighty." Evangelist Bamosotla continued: "In the morning, just when the sun had risen, we found that the chief had just finished drinking the fourth bottle of *khadi*!" He paused for a while to allow the congregation to finish laughing and then continued:

"When the trial started, just after Kgwengweng had reported how much we had contaminated the water, *khadi* started doing the unspeakable in the chief. His eyes were concealed under a huge cap that he wore. As we were trying to explain to him and giving him all the explanations that we had given Kgwengweng and his men at the stream, he was already yawning with some saliva even dripping out of his mouth. He was dead asleep and dreaming. When he woke up from his slumber, he instructed us to disperse and mentioned that he was going to send his people to take us to Molepolole. We waited for him to do that but he didn't up to this day. Then, later we heard that the men who had been sent to fetch us had run away claiming that they feared the God of Motlha-o-Etla church."

The whole congregation erupted into a joyous celebration:

"Amen! Hallelujah! Glory be to the Lord"

"I have even returned here but still I haven't heard from them. God's power is amazing brothers. The hostile enemies turn into crazy people when they see the Lord. Now his work is back to normal. And, the congregation in Lephephe sends warm greetings."

Bamosotla concluded like that and then sat down. As for the congregation, it erupted with a hymn and the service continued.

****

As time passed, Rre Tlholego got very sad. This world is indeed coming to an end. What used to be human is now nothing but foolishness. The newly converted look at things in a different way. Our ancestors now mean nothing to them. They are just stepping on them using their feet. Really, where is this younger generation headed to? When we talk of the earth we don't just mean the soil and stones on it, but also the humans who occupy it. The life and death of humans is determined by their conduct. When, for example, everyone in a homestead has good manners, that makes a perfect family. When families are perfect that makes a strong clan. If the clans are powerful they build a stable and perfect nation. A nation is a cart of cattle. When one person is reluctant, the whole nation becomes weak in terms of progress. The conduct of a nation is like water filled in a dam. At times this water sits so still and reflects like a mirror. But the day it dries out the only thing that is left is mud where tadpoles are trapped and dying. All the waters that had protected life would have been soaked by the soil to the extent that the life of all the water species fades into the stench of mud.

Rre Tlholego wondered if Modiko's bad conduct, which he displayed in front of the chief the other day is an example of the drying manner or he is just being a poor naive child who has been deceived by rebellious adults. He then concluded that it was about time that he went with Modiko to the hill to go and look for the herb that he had long wanted to find. Because the plants had grown, it was going to be an easy find. They should have gone to look for this herb during the month of *tebatsa-barwaledi* but he kept on getting busy every time he wanted to go there. It was now the perfect time for him to go.

The sun-sizzle of that Saturday met them when they were about to pass Bojikwi's house. Just like all the other homesteads belonging to the Boers, cars were packed everywhere making it hard for one to walk. One car packed after another.

"This Boer is the only one who is a great mechanic. As for others they are just garbage. Ever since he fixed my car, it has never given me any problems," Rre Tlholego said while simultaneously using his rod to point.

Modiko asked, "But is he better than Van Jan? I heard that one is the best."

"Wai! That deceives people with paint only. Jane does not do much but after that he paints the car tyres with red paint and for that reason people will think that the car is new. Drive it, before you even pass Motanka it is already crumbling."

They walked in silence until they crossed the river. When they were by Matlotse's yard Rre Tlholego then said:

"Mokgaodi had invited me to go with him to his niece's wedding. I realized that if I go I will not find time to get the herb that we are going to look for."

"Grandfather, what is it that makes people get married so much in August? Just recently one of the Whitemen who teaches us asked me this question but I wasn't sure of how I must answer him," Modiko asked with a curious face.

The old man lit his pipe and smoked it with all his strength. Three clouds of smoke were sent to the atmosphere where they evaporated to the sky. He coughed and then spit, *jwatlaka!*

"First of all, during this month, everyone is home to run the necessary errands. Also, people need helpers, those who can help them hold the plough during the ploughing season. Secondly, they are doing the will of our ancestors, our forefathers. You will realize that during this month, things are created anew. Look at the green plants and other seedlings sprouting from the earth. Even the donkeys, frogs and birds it is time for the earth to reproduce." He smoked his pipe, again.

"Well I didn't even realize that." Modiko said with noticeable happiness and one of a kind that showed he was excited to learn new lessons that opened his mind.

At this point, the old man was the one leading the walk. He was about to climb up the slanted terrain of the hill. As they moved up the hill it was very easy to see the entire village. All the way from Tshwaanyane river to where Motanka and Thaone rivers meet like thighs that suspend a thick body of Tshwaanayane. Sitting next to these rivers is the houses of the Boers which glow with corrugated iron roofs. On top of each roof, the thick stones are neatly packed to prevent the roof from falling due to wind. Further from these houses lies Thaone dam. The still waters of *sephai* rains have filled the banks of the dam. The acacia trees have decorated the stream which flows into this dam. It is as if the water is pumped forcefully from the hills. From the stem of the hill to the deepness of the river, the ancestors are showing off their miracles. The colorful butterflies sit atop the spread of the green grass and the blend of their colors compares with the skin of a zebra. Unripe *mmilo* and *mmupudu* wildfruits are surrounded by big beautiful butterflies. The breath of life filled their noses.

"Medicine is what gives us our identity. Without it there's no life," Rre Tlholego remarked to which Modiko affirmed.

"It is true *rra*." Poor Modiko was thinking about what his teacher taught him at school, that green plants were the source of life. It is as if they sit betwixt human life and death. However, Rre Tlholego was thinking about something else and clearly not what Modiko was thinking about. He therefore continued as if he didn't pay attention to what his grandson had said,

"When a baby is born, we welcome him to earth using *modi*[4] from a tree. Every aspect of human life, marriage, kraal, land and health we use *modi* for protection." He put his pipe back in one of the pockets of his coat.

---

[4] Literal translation: "root"

"*Modi* can even control thunder. The giant snakes from the rocks capable of killing any human who comes their path lie sullen and lethargic when *modi* is clotting all of their blood. All the strength from the ancestors is revealed through *modi* from a tree. I don't know what you Christians say about this."

With these words the old man knew he had opened a conversation.

"Pastor Mmolaaditso said Jesus is the only person whom we have to rely on. He is the strength of a Christian. He is both the shield and the spear for anyone who is a Christian. Jesus is more powerful than the root from a tree, he just says through the word and then miracles happen," Modiko said.

They were now walking in the middle of the bush and it was easy to spot stones here and there which made it easy to forget that they were in fact walking at the top of the mountain. Rre Tlholego wa leading the walk and used both of his hands to hold a hoe which they were to use for digging. It sat across both of his shoulders. He realized that Modiko was getting too excited to talk but he then decided not to talk to him about Jesus or Christianity. It is better for him to meander like an ant that attempts to test how hot the ash is.

"Have you ever stood in front of the congregation to teach?"

"Yes *Rra*. About twice."

"Oh, so in your church everyone can preach? I was under the impression that pastors are the only ones who teach," Rre Tlholego said.

"That only happens at Lovelace's church, because they like to keep the scriptures a secret. They don't want the followers to read for themselves and teach others."

They walked for some time until just after they had derailed from the thin walking path where they reached a thick bush. At that time, they began seeing bones and skulls of dead animals. The bones were very white, and it was clear that the flesh was devoured and later the remaining part of the bone was washed clean by rain water. A strong smell filled the atmosphere. It smelled like a decomposed dog and some wild flowers therefore making a mixture of both a stench and a scent. Soon the flies also filled the open space, and they fled into their faces. As for them, they walked in deep silence except for noise from the movement of their footsteps.

Modiko looked sideways showing fear and confusion. He walked much closer to his grandfather and he was walking so closely that he kept slipping on his feet. His grandfather noticed fear that had consumed Modiko and at this point he knew very well that finally his ancestors were giving him an answer.

"Young man, have you ever heard of *sephatsiphatsi*?"

"No *Rra*! Yes *Rra*!...." Modiko responded, but before he could continue Rre Tlholego interrupted him.

"Yes-No!! Which one should I take for an answer? Why do you have so many words as if your deep tooth is being removed? I asked, do you know *sephatsiphatsi*?"

"I have only heard of it, never seen it before."

Modiko's voice was shaking and Rre Tlholego noticed this so he knew his plan was going to work as intended. He then asked,

"So those who told you about it, what did they say? What does it look like?"

Modiko swallowed a thump that had blocked his throat. He licked both of his lips like a goat that just came off from the sorghum field. His voice had even changed and at this time he spoke with a rather thinly, trembling and constrained voice. If you knew how he speaks, it was easy to decipher the voice didn't sound like it was his.

"They said it is ugly."

"What kind of ugliness? Is it marred with excrement?"

"They said only evil things live there. It is an abomination to talk about them."

Modiko said while looking on each direction quite relentlessly.

The thick *lengana* trees merged to make the bush even much darker. The number of dead bones had now increased making that place to look like a butchery. Shockingly, there was no evidence of human footprints on the ground even that of wild animals or cattle. His body cringed, and it felt like ants were crawling all over his naked body. He felt his skin moving itself, like the way a cow skin would move when it tries to scare the flies away from a position where the swinging of its tail cannot reach. He shrunk, again. He wanted to tell his grandfather that they must go back.

The thin wind that had formed hit their faces right in front. Along with it came a quite stench which forced its way into their noses. As always, Rre Tlholego did not hesitate to spit in response. The wind then picked dried debris in its path. It pulled off the old man's hat and hung it atop the mongana tree. When that happened, grey hair was left exposed with some black hair here and there. They struggled to remove the hat from the tree. After they succeeded, Rre Tlholego spotted a spread rock and noticed Modiko's eyes which were pleading without saying for them to go back home.

"Young man," He called.

"*Rra.*" Modiko answered.

"You know you were just numb when I asked what you know about *sephatsiphatsi*. But let's leave it at that. When you talk about something over and over again, it ends up losing its essence. I will tell you, and you will also get to see it yourself because it is not far from here. When we arrive, you will see a smooth stone that shines like water. We might find huge snakes that live in these rocks basking in the sun. These are not snakes, they are our ancestors. At the head you will see the head of an old man who has whitened hair and beard, but with the body of a large snake. This is the condition that our forefathers exist in. But for you to see them, and be able to live to tell the story the next day, you need to be prepared using their *lonaka*. It is required that at this time *modi* protects you. But now I really don't know what will happen if you have been protected by Jesus like you claimed earlier. Anyway, let's go."

They stopped.

They walked for a while when Modiko began pulling his uncle's coat at the back.

"Grandfather let's wait here first. I am very scared. Please let's not go there."

"Are you the one who can even say that? We are supposed to dig some herbs for your grandmother near *sephatsiphatsi*. Jesus will defeat the ancestors. Is that not true? I want you to see true nature, so that when you destroy it, at least you would have seen it first. Let's go young man and don't waste time."

The sun was just above their heads when they arrived near *sephatsiphatsi.*

"I don't want to offend the ancestors, but I want you to see what is enough."

They climbed up the hill and watched the spreading view of a strikingly shiny surface. The rock shone in a perplexing way. Modiko looked at it with shock. The rock had spread the size of a very huge field. It looked like a big lake. The only thing that was different about it was the way it shone because it there is so much water in the surface, it should appear bluish and therefore could not shine in the way it did. He heard that Modiko was in fact shaking but he overlooked him anyway and said:

"That rock is the one that attracts cattle and other wild animals. They come here deceived into thinking this is water but then the huge snakes will kill them. The bones that you can see here belong to animals that were dying of thirst."

Modiko breathed loudly. But he did not say anything.

"Now, no man or animal can come to this place."

Rre Tlholego continued,

"It is the mouth of Ojang. We are only able to stand here because we have been protected by our forefathers, bo-Letlotla, one whose totem is a crocodile. The son of Modiko of Mooketsa, of deep rivers, a river without a stumble. The only thing that can stumble one in this river is the sand. It is a thigh with spots from the heavy stings of a bee. *Ka fa go makodi-kodi kafa mapawa mapalamo a boramothekge.*"

Rre Tlholego said while watching the *sephatsiphatsi* with deep commitment of emotion. His eyes had thinned, and he kept on massaging his beard. He then turned to Modiko and stared at him as if he was reading his heart and mind. As for Modiko, he looked the other side like someone who was guilty of something. Rre Tlholego coughed and cleared his throat. Sputum came out of his mouth with heavy energy such that it coiled itself with the dust.

"Let's go," Rre Tlholego said.

They returned using the same road path they came walking through. After they left the thick *lengana* bush Rre Tlholego, upon hearing that Modiko was now feeling at ease, said,

"Have you now seen *Sephatsiphatsi?*"

Modiko then licked his lip and answered,

"Yes *Rra*. All this time I have just been hearing stories about it. It is such a scary place."

"Actually, you haven't seen anything yet," Tlholego responded. "At times you will find pieces of biltong hanging from the tree. If you take them home they turn into big snakes. If that happens, you can only live if the ancestors love you. If not you will just vanish like a locust. This boy, the son of Ketlaabareng, died that kind of death. The same thing happened to Rapula."

The day had almost gone when they arrived at the end of the hill. They found a lot of herb that they were looking for. Traditional doctors call it *Phate-tse-dintsho*. It is a small green plant with red flowers. It grows at mostly at the edge of the hill and at its top.

"Young man, this medicine heals every sickness suffered by our women," Rre Tlholego said while removing some stones so that he could start digging. "Over that side of the hill by the village it no longer grows. Some of these amateur medicine men have finished it."

"Is the only one that can heal women ailments?" Modiko probed.

"Of course not, but this one is the best. It heals the womb, infertility and all other kinds of diseases."

"How is it used?"

"Owaii! Young man it seems like you want to know everything. Do you want to become a *ngaka?*"

Rre Tlholego laughed and patted Modiko on his shoulder. He was obviously pleased to see Modiko was showing interest in his tradition.

Chapter 11

The old man, Rre Tlholego wanted to say something that he had long wanted to discuss. If you want a cyst to heal, the only solution is to cut it open than to scare the flies away using a leaf or smear it with some oil. He had been waiting for a long time for this boy to grow up and reach maturity. Now the ancestors had answered his plea. They have grown up the young man and now the very same child he was talking about is right at the heart of hill with him, digging traditional herbs.

"*Monnanyana!*"

"*Rra*" Modiko answered.

"I think we have gathered enough, we can now take a break and then go back." Rre Tlholego said while taking a hoe from Modiko who at the time was helping him to dig. They sat on the rocks. He pulled out a thorn from a nearby tree and used it to remove another one that had pricked him on the palm of his hand.

They had set at the top of the mountain but at its southern boundary. It was easy to spot some small rivers that drew the water from this hill. Like the veins of a white person the rivers looked green because of the vegetation that surrounded it with plenty of *mokgalo* trees. There were many other tree species like *leokana, lega, lengana* and, *letlhajwa* that sat on its beautiful margins. It was also easy to see the dispersed acacia trees that swayed boastfully in the area. It was clear that such were grown by the ancestors in their natural esteem. The hornbills and grey louries flew atop the white flowers as they chirped, *koeeee*! That's when Modiko remembered pastor Ramarepetla who when he prayed used to claim that even birds like the grey louries like to praise the creator when they chirp.

There were a few pebbles here and there in the open space where cactus share the same place with *mosu* trees. Not very far from the hill there is Magagarape's lands.

Rre Tlholego was in deep thought, again. His eyes had thinned as he looked at the rains that looked as if they dangled on dew. He then started talking;

"Do you see those rocks over there?" He pointed.

"Yes, those ones over there," Modiko answered.

"The rocks are in Thamaga. Do you know how that village got its name?"

"No *rra*, I don't know. I only know that the people who come from there are called Bakgatla of Mmanaana. I also heard that because of their cowardice they tied a leash to a calf with reddish-brown and white marks on its skin to deceive their foes."

"Yes, I know about that too. But I don't think that was cowardly. It was a good strategy. A mosquito once told an elephant that a battle is not for the gigantic only, it is about strategy. When the elephant disagreed, the mosquito went straight into his trunk. So these Bakgatla were in fact putting their enemies in their place by just being strategic."

"You were just about to tell me how Thamaga got its name," Modiko reminded his grandfather.

"Oh, I almost forgot. It's a long story."

He said as he used his folding his knife to remove dirt from his pipe. After filling it up with tobacco he lit it and then smoked it. Five clouds of smoke were sent to the clouds. They smelled like burning chicken droppings. He then continued:

"Thamaga got its name after our battle with Paul's boers. I was still a young boy at the time, about the same age as Moalosi. The Boers came and they were led by Paul, who was chasing after the Bakgatla of Mmanaana. With his red angry eyes, Paul told our King that he was looking for Bakgatla. But then *Mmabatho* told the Boer that the Bakgatla that he was looking for were in his stomach. He then went ahead and asked him to cut open his belly to take them out if he likes. Paul got angry but our King was done talking. But that happened long time back, when our traditional leaders had not converted to these churches."

"Due to anger, the Boer declared war. He was intending to grab all of the cattle belonging to the Bakwena. What a lie! A kind of lie that can cause one to be struck by thunder at daylight. The Bakwena defeated the Boers using that *lekgwapha* over there. You see this one, it really saved us during difficult times. The Boers were sitting on top of that tree over there. Can you see it?"

"Yes *Rra*," Modiko responded.

"They were up there. The Bakwena men plucked all the leaves from these trees and suspended them using logs. After that they clothed them with coats. Then each men waited by next to it. The trees were also given the hats such that when the Boers saw that they were shocked and thought that Bakwena had outnumbered them."

Modiko could not hold off from laughing. Rre Tlholego spit, again, *jwatlaka!* He held his chin.

"When the Boers fired, the tree stood still. Second time, the coat slightly moved but the posture still stood erect. They got carried away and thought that the third shot would in fact finish him off. As a result, the Boers spent the whole day fighting the trees, mekgwapha trees. As for the Bakwena they sat on the margins of that rock waiting for the right time. That is why that place is called Seokomedi, meaning a concealed place from where one peers. It is where our enemies were stalked."

"When the Boers were now very tired, somebody said 'now is the right time to retaliate and shoot.' And then all the men who were hiding came out from their hiding places and pounced on the Boers. Kitiii! Kitiii! One shot and a Boer was down. Immediately someone would refill the gunpowder and keep shooting. Their leader was a Mokwena man called Raditsebe. The *Ngaka* had instructed that after the battle they must bring to him a pointing finger from one of the Boers. Raditsebe breathed into the bones during divination. He praised himself as a fighter, and from his hiding place aimed exactly at Paul's pointing finger. He knew very well that that was the finger that made him do crazy things. He ripped off Paul's pointing finger."

"Paul was heard screaming like a goat that cannot endure the pain of castration. When the other Boers saw that their leaders was the one screaming and crying in deep pain, they all left and ran away for their lives. At this point, Paul dragged himself to his horse which had reddish-brown and white marks. Some of the horses owned by the Boers left running but it was over that hill where Paul's horse died. Because of this particular incident, the place acquired its name literally being named after this horse."

"Ehe! Ou! Banna!" Modiko responded in obvious shock. His grandfather continued and asked

"But come to think of it this way, what do you think caused the Boers to spend the entire day fighting trees?"

"No, I have no idea at all. Could it be possible that it is because they were far so they could not see clearly?" Modiko.

"No, it is medicine. Like I told you, *modi* from a tree is very powerful. The Bakwena use it from this big *kgogela*, a huge snake from the river. Our *ngaka* only breaths into the air using his breath and then everything that follows is mystery. The midst will immediately fill the atmosphere and blind the Boers. They can only see darkness while we are stalking them from our hiding place. The power of *modi* comes from the ancestors, our forefathers. When the Boers attacked us, they surely had their gods too, but those of our forefathers defeated them."

"What exactly are the ancestors or *badimo* as you say? How are they different from the God that we worship from our church? Our pastor has told us that these badimo are idols which the bible is admonishing us against their worship." Modiko asked.

At this point, Rre Tlholego knew that it was time for him to enlighten his grandson. It was as if he was cutting a portion of a watermelon for him. The fact of the matter is that it is impossible to arrive at the heart of the watermelon without first cutting through its outer part. Therefore, the idea of telling his boy about these wars between the Bakwena and the Boers was a way of laying a foundation for what he wanted to tell the boy. He put his pipe aside and then said:

"*Badimo* are our ancestors, our forefathers and great grandparents who died a long time ago. There is a mighty God who controls *badimo* to take the instructions and initiate what he wants them to do such as making rain, growing sorghum and other plants to grow. When we want rain, the King, who represents Badimo on earth goes to make an offering at the bush in the same way when we go for hunting or letsema. When we get there, we appease and plead with our ancestors to give us rain. In return, they ask for us on behalf of God. That is how it is. The churches use the same concept. There is God. And then there are ancestors of the Jewish and the Whites. When we went to fight during the war, white people with whom we fought alongside talked to us a lot about a certain Jewish woman called Mary. They also talked of Peter, John and Paul. These people are said to be the anointed ones. Even today they still talk about them even though they died many years ago. When your father starts a prayer he mentions Abraham, Isaac and, Jacob. Just ask any random Jew, they will not hesitate to tell you that they have blood relations with Abraham."

"The reason why there are many nations on this earth, each one of them worship the God of their ancestors. That is why I am saying you have abandoned the gods of your forefathers and followed the gods of other nations."

Rre Tlholego kept quiet for some time looking at the thick bush and lekgwapha trees that helped them to defeat the Boers. He knew that his silence would make his words sink like rain water in the soil. When he noticed that Modiko was busy digesting what he told him he asked a question.

"Do you know what has made us to abandon our religion, our traditions, and our identity and then followed visitors who are not even interested in learning our language?"

"No, I don't know," Modiko responded wanting to hear what his grandfather had to say.

"A white man came to us with some tricks. Yes indeed, he came with deceit. Listen to me properly. First when he came he was preaching peace and friendship to us. We welcomed him warmly thinking that he was just hungry and passing by. We gave him some food and after he finished eating, his belly filled, he took out the bible. From the bible he told us about God and his son who was capable of making all the porridge in this basin to raise and feed all the people living in Molepolole. This was a man who is said to know his tricks very well that he can walk on top of the large body of water on his barefoot without sinking. As we were listening to all this we saw a

101

Whiteman flying a metallic bird atop our plains and roofs. *Mogalammakapa!* We thought this must be a very powerful man indeed. His God must be quite stronger than ours."

"Then secondly, he came with a rifle. He can smoke an enemy from a very far distance. When his enemy tries to come closer to him so he can stab him using a spear he just fires a bullet and the enemy dies instantly. The Whiteman then promised us that if we give him a piece of land to grow crops and another one where he can build a place of worship then he will in return teach us his tricks. We then gave him the land and allowed him to build his place of worship amongst us. By the way, by so doing we were ignoring the advice of our ancestors. Our ancestors had long warned, using a *ngaka*, that since the times of Lowe and Bile, a man with a different skin color will come from the blue waters. They also said that one should be fought because he was going to steal our land."

Rre Tlholego used his hand to kill a horsefly that was sucking blood on his hand. He smashed it once such that it fell onto the ground. Immediately, ants started dragging it to their hole. He then poured some soil from where he was bitten to stop blood from coming out.

"This is how Ramolaisi's religion found its way into Bakwena. Most of them were converted and they started following this new religion. Now the white pastors are giving all the young men who were converted a responsibility to preach. Bakwena are even taking new names. Your father just got converted recently. This church of yours Motlha-o-Etla was found just recently here in Molepolole. It was introduced by a certain man named Lefoko who comes from Matlhalerweng ward. Then your father joined and decided to abandon his Setswana name Mokganedi and started calling himself Jeremiah. Mmolaaditso called himself Jonah. Most of the converts abandoned their birth names given to them by their parents and took ones from the bible.

Even those people who were doctors, they threw away their *dipheko* and started saying that their *pheko* was Jesus. We saw the inevitable. People leaving behind their identity and following the foreign things. The clay pots and beer calabashes were broken and thrown away.

Traditional beer became a taboo. What is shocking is that they drink alcohol during the Passover. When they are sick they can only go to Dr. Lovelace, everything in Setswana tradition is a sin to them. This is the same omen of abomination that once killed a head louse."

The old man moved backwards from a rock where he was sitting on and then continued:

"A head louse once had a conversation with another one usually found on clothes. The one in the head was ashamed of its blackness. It then asked the body louse what it must do to look whiter like the body louse. It wanted to look like the head louse especially after sucking blood so that it looks red like summer flowers.

The body louse suggested to the head louse that it was better for him to quench himself and bath in boiling water. That would in return remove its black color. Blindly, the body louse listened and then jumped into boiling water and died. Any creature that tries to transform itself from how the ancestors created it will die."

He coughed, actually not to cough in the strict sense, but he cleared his throat. He glanced at his friend and discovered that he was deeply engrossed in what he told him. It was evident that he was thinking deeply about the matter.

"I am telling you these things because I know you are very intelligent towards these modern things. I just wanted to help you so that you know that as you are following this English culture, you should not forget your tradition and come to look like a head louse."

"This is the real thing that I wanted to tell you. You know that Letlotla gave birth to two boys, being Mosiami and myself. Mosiami gave birth to your aunt, Mma Kelereng, and your father Mokganedi. Unfortunately, the old man died. Now, because your father frequented his visits to Gauteng when he was still a young man, I became the leader of this Kgotla of Dikoloi. I am just holding this position for him in the meantime. Am I clear?"

"Yes *Rra*."

"Now when your father was already as old as he is now, I gathered all the people to hand over the leadership to him. This was at the time when he was already converted into Motlha-o-Etla. He refused. He said that the kingdom of this earth rots and as for him he wanted to preserve his on heaven. Since that time I have been looking at you and hoping that you will not disappoint me the way he did. I am also hoping that you will not disappoint the ancestors. If I was like other people, by now I would be very happy as I would have passed this position to one of my children. But I am a human being, my grandchild. I am not like a pig which we like to say it is one animal that doesn't even know what makes it fat because it has a habit of just eating everything. Our ancestors are not foolish, they cannot be deceived. Not even for a bit. So my child will you take the leadership of the Dikoloi ward?"

Modiko felt the sadness that was consuming him. He felt an emotional pain ripping him off from his ribs up to the eardrum. He then said:

"Grandfather, I am still very young. Give me some time to think about it first. I want to finish my school first."

"That's a good answer. Think about it first and please don't offend our ancestors my son. When are you finishing school?"

"I am just left with two years and then I will be done."

"What level are you at your school by the way?"

"I'm doing standard seven. Then after that I will proceed to do form one."

"Form one? Too much education will make you go crazy."

"No *rra*, education does not make one mad. There are people who are actually more educated than me but they are not mad."

It took them sometime conversing about education but before he knew it Rre Tlholego was back engaging him in serious talk again. He asked Modiko

"So, my grandchild how did you become a Christian?"

Modiko took some time before he answered the question. It seemed as if what was in his mind was going to be a very long story. Modiko began responding to Rre Tlholego's question. A lump blocked his throat and tears were visible in his eyes while the old man listened, although he also could not hold back his emotions. He looked at Modiko with a sense of pity. And, because he knew the kind of life that

Modiko's father imposed on him Rre Tlholego could not hold off his tears. But thankfully they managed to hold them. He himself had seen more persecutions than this one during the war when he was a conscript. The amount of animosity and heartlessness that people commit on other humans is far worse and brutal than those done by wild animals.

Chapter 12

It is the land without sunshine. There people just live in constant darkness. Big mountains form a chain but at the same time they are sprung separately like fetching eggs of a snake. The trees there stand erect. And thumps of white grass can be spotted here and there like teeth in the mouth of an old woman. Distantly, there sits a shiny hill with the color of a millipede, but there is no life there, except for its shine.

The darkness is devoured by the light from the burning fire of an abyss. No one really knows the depth of this abyss. And no one would dare want to know how deep it is. The heat from this dungeon can be felt by someone from a very far distance. The fire burns persistently like a pile of branches with very dry debris. There is black smoke that has filled the atmosphere. Its flame is a mixture of red, blue and the color of an egg yolk. Sitting next to this fire is a giant of a man with the posture and gait of a baboon. His limbs are very long and thick like a pestle from Mmangwato. His lips match that of a careless baboon, and his teeth are like that of a big dog. The neck and body are combined such that it is it hard to tell the difference. The rest of the body is green fur. Protruding from his head are two sharp horns, although they are not too long, almost looking like that of a child. This man-baboon also has a very long tail. His feet and hands look like paws which have claws of an eagle or cock. This man is also holding on his hand a long fork with three sharp teeth. He uses this fork to grill bodies that are burning inside this abyss.

Flying in the open sky are creatures that look like monkeys in terms of their size. However, they flew using the wings of bats. The open sky grew even darker as these creatures kept on increasing in number. Their eyes emitted some glittering light. The kind of noise that they made was very scary and indeed extremely frightening. When they stopped crying it produced the disturbing noise of the sound of water pumping out of a gallon. Giant millipedes could be spotted in the area.

They were very huge that it is fitting to compare them with the size of a well grown horse. Their feet have many gullies and portions.

Radikhwaere, as he should be called, looks like a baboon-man. It is hard to tell if he is man or baboon. However, he is much bigger in size. His chest is big but he has a very thin waist, which makes him look disproportional. Another difference is that instead of paws, he has a hoofed feet. His mouth looks like that of a dog and it is very red inside like a lizard that catches a fly. His teeth too, are red and they can be compared to that of a dog that has just drank blood or a wild dog that just finished feasting on its prey.

He barked using his thundering voice. In response the flying monkeys that had bat wings began harassing the atmosphere. That's when the real work started. The monkey like creatures came holding a very fat woman who at the time was crying persistently like a baby who stepped on a glowing coal:

"*Ijo!* Poverty is such a painful thing. Please let me go back to the earth to repent. *Ijoo!!*"

The creatures just brought the woman to the burning abyss and therefore ignoring what she was pleading for. At once he stabbed her right in between her shoulders using a fork and blood splashed as if it was coming out of a thin hose pipe. The baboon like man then lifted her up and took her to the fire. This poor woman could no longer cry out loudly like before. He threw her into the fire and immediately there was a spark from where she was thrown. They were carried into the atmosphere where they later diffused into the spread of the dark sky.

Her eyes blasted rather loudly, and the atmosphere was filled with the smell of her roasted and calloused flesh. The creatures were already bringing their second victim. He was a very thin man whom it was easy to assume that he must have been sick from tuberculosis. This one was just thrown without much energy or effort put to it, unlike with that woman. He was sunk into the fiery abyss in silence. The work continued like that until there was only one person left. They held this one too, with their fiery eyes. Modiko screamed very loudly. They pulled him to the fire and even though he was a good distance away from this abyss he was already feeling the scorch of the fire. He screamed even louder. *Radikhaere* and a baboon man came to him. He was grabbed by his neck by one of them. Both of their hands were bloody and scaly. He was then taken to an abyss with an unquenchable fire. Even though he had not been thrown in, the heat was already peeling off his skin. A time came when he was finally to be thrown into an abyss but that's when he screamed to a point of waking up his father. In response, his father shook him angrily.

"Wake up, why are you disturbing me like this?" Evangel Letlotla barked.

Modiko woke up from his sleep. He was shaking and sweating profusely. He looked at his father in the eyes, obviously confused by anger.

"What's your problem?" His father asked.

"I had a nightmare of Satan throwing me into a fire," Modiko lamented.

"It is because of your sins. I have long begged you to get baptized since when? The Lord was warning you for the last time," The evangel Jeremiah Letlotla said.

Rre Tlholego listened attentively as Modiko told him about things that are in Seokomedi hills. But his question was, "So, is that the only reason you got baptized?"

"*Yes Rra,* the fright and the confusion put pressure on me in order to escape the abyss."

"Are you still afraid of that abyss?"

"Yes, very much. That picture really scared me when I was young. Sometimes I would hide it or flip it when my father went to the field," Modiko told.

"Your nightmarish dream was because of this picture. In other words, you were coerced into your religion because you feared the fire. I can see that now. You are now held captive like most of them. But the words that I told you my grandchild, before it is too late do not throw away your tradition. The Dikoloi clan is yours."

Modiko and his grandfather gathered their herbs and medicine and put them inside a skunk skin sac and then left. As they walked back home, Rre Tlholego broke the silence:

"I personally don't believe that Satan exists. There is nothing like that. Satan is nothing but poverty. But you know poverty can cause you so much stress to a point of talking through your heart. It makes you even want to bewitch those who are hardworking and successful. This is what being Satanic is. But as for the creature with a long tail that we are supposed to believe that it is Satan, no ways! A Whiteman has used this concept of Satan on us in the same way that we use '*gogo*' to scare young children. That is the plain truth and nothing beyond that."

They left the hills when the day was about to end, almost in between very late afternoon and evening. The dark shadows had formed, and they were very hungry. Modiko's stomach grumbled and he felt as if worms were eating away his bowels. Over a distance from where they were they spotted two men underneath *morolwana* trees. From where they were sitting there was also some smoke coming out from there. It penetrated through the thick branches of the tree.

"Let's go to them and see what they are doing," Rre Tlholego said. They went right and crossed through the grass that was huge and dry. When they walked, the grass broke underneath their feet and made some noise and dust at the same time. As they came closer they realized that the men were skinning a cow.

"The land of the Bakwena is so big and spreading, I really wonder where you are coming from Rramodisaemang?" Mohamed asked Rre Tlholego almost immediately after they exchanged greetings.

"Now where did you get this *lekgowa*?" He asked while looking at Modiko.

"We are coming from the hills over there. You know my children are not well. So, we wanted to go and dig some medicine to stop the pains. Yes, I want to show this young man our traditional way of life which he was born and raised in. Not the talk of '*haejini*' and '*ente*' which belong to other people's cultures."

"You are doing very well uncle. A person is what he is because of his tradition. A bat is said to have been in a huge inner conflict during the battle because he was unsure of whose side to take," Mohammed remarked.

Mohammed had this name because he was named after a certain Indian who sold his parents a good concoction that healed him when he was still young. They had tried taking the child to all the traditional doctors they knew but nothing changed. But immediately after this medicine was bought within a short period the child was playing and fully recovered although he was very sick.

"Now what's wrong with this cow?" Rre Tlholego asked.

"It got trapped in the mud, we have found it long dead."

"Cut a piece of liver to roast it for me quickly. I spent the whole day without eating anything. We left very early in the morning and there is literally nothing in my stomach," Rre Tlholego asked.

Mohammed removed it and placed it on top of a hot glowing coal. When Modiko saw this he remembered Rre Ramaologa who died a while back. When he was still alive he asked Modiko and some of the boys to look after his roasted ox liver while he rushed to his compound. After it was well cooked one of the boys came up with an idea that they must eat the ox liver because they well knew that Ramaologa was not going to give them anything, even a small piece about the size of the head of a millipede.

Modiko then took the liver and hid it by the blanket. Ramaologa closed his left nostril using his thumb and then forced the dark mucus out. He did the same with the left nose. He then used his fingers to clean his nose and rubbed palms against each other. His eyes were focused at the place where he had left the ox liver roasting.

"Young men, where is the liver?" He asked with his eyes almost wide opened like that of a mad goat.

"There is another man who came here and took it," Modiko responded.

"Where is he?"

"He went there, over there," Modiko pointed using his finger.

"What is his name?"

"We don't know him."

Ramaologa licked his lips. He looked at Modiko.

"When we are eating *mokoto* you must sit by my side so that you can show him to me," Ramaologa fumed.

"I will show him the bitterness of the herb." *Nxa!* He expressed his annoyance and then left.

As for Modiko and his friends, they ate the ox liver. And again, when time for *mokoto* arrived Modiko enjoyed so much meat because he was pretending to be watching for the man who stole Ramaologa's ox liver. Ramaologa finally gave up when Modiko told him that he couldn't find the man who stole the ox liver.

After the liver from Mohammed's cow had roasted and was well cooked, Rre Tlholego removed his knife and cut a piece for Modiko.

"Take this my grandchild, even if it is well cooked just eat it. It is often said that a pig doesn't know what makes it fat."

Modiko shook his head. "I have been instructed not to eat meat from dead animals," Modiko exclaimed.

Rre Tlholego and other men who were there were very shocked. They looked at Modiko as if he was a dog that had lost its mind therefore trying to bite its own tail. Rre Tlholego then said

"Who said that?"

"The bible says that. Pastor Mmolaaditso too has said that. He read for us these words from the bible."

"So now do you eat the cow while it is alive? Are you wild dogs?" Mohammed asked. Other men, including Rre Tlholego, laughed. Modiko was left embarrassed and ashamed. Another man who was at this point using an axe to cut the ribs then said

"Old man, this young man will die of hunger. Just enjoy your liver and leave him alone. He will eat the bible. Is this Mmolaaditso that he is talking about not the one from the Motlhaoetla church?"

"That's the one. We heartlessly killed people together during the war. The type of meat that we ate at the time we didn't know whether it came from a cow that had just died or that was slaughtered first," Rre Tlholego answered.

The man who was ripping off the ribs with an axe continued telling the story of what he knew about Mmolaaditso.

"These pastors of yours are deceiving you. They keep saying do this, do that. However, they keep doing the exact things that they instruct you not to do. Just last year, their cow, Romeisi, died. He ate it and I witnessed it and I am not basing this in a hearsay. I have also heard that the members of the Motlhaoetla church don't drink alcohol, they don't smoke and they don't even use traditional medicine. Mmolaaditso drinks alcohol. He pours that stuff that looks like urine in a kettle and drinks it so that it looks as if he is having tea without milk. He is able to hold that church of his because of *modi*. His ngaka is called Mogatla wa Phepheng. That one is not a traditional doctor, he is a wizard. You know them very well the Bakgatla of Mmanaana. They can cause a *tladi* or thunder to strike you even in a cloudless sky."

"I was just telling my grandson that every Motswana was born with *modi*. No matter how one tries to become like a head louse he can never change to be what he is not. I'm therefore not surprised that Mmolaaditso has become a hypocrite, saying this but meaning that. He knows what he is doing, he is just getting the money for himself to fill his belly. You can see the man who eats well by just looking at his belly. His belly is big because he is eating well. He is very smart. He knows that *maano go sita a loso*. He does not use the tithes and other contributions from the church to build a church like Ramolaisi. The women who have converted to his church mix the soil to decorate his compound. This boy is very smart," Rre Tlholego said happily, while laughing at the same time.

All this time Modiko had been listening to what the men were saying but didn't really believe that they were telling the truth. So, he decided not to say anything. That's the only way of reading between the lies of a talkative person, he thought naively.

Their walk from where the cow was skinned by the river did not have any interesting incidents. The old man was full after having eaten so much beef. He even took some of the meat for himself and hung it on one of the sharp sticks he had picked. The old man knew very well what was happening.

Therefore, he did not attempt to engage Modiko in a conversation because he knew that a hungry man is usually very short tempered. They went just like that in silence, no one saying anything. Modiko was the one holding a bag that carried the medicinal plants while Rre Tlholego carried a hoe, and of course, the meat that he took from that place. By this time, Modiko was increasingly growing impatient especially when the old man kept stopping frequently to greet the people that he met on the way.

They passed the gullies near Goodinti and after they walked for some kilometers they spotted Evangel Letlotla's house. It looked different from the other houses that were located near it. It was plastered with soil but built using bricks and cement. Its corrugated iron roof shone and compelled any passerby to look at it. On that Saturday, the evangelist had hired people to do some renovations in the house using cement and cow dung. He was painting the door and windows in blue, the color of the sky. That was his favourite color. This is the kind of color that the Children of Israel found in Canaan. He liked to say that when he was happy.

As they got closer to his father's home, Modiko asked Rre Tlholego to take the bag that had medicines before his father saw him. Rre Tlholego did that at once and he knew very well why. His instincts told him that something was surely going to happen. Before the end of the day he would have heard something about this.

They stopped by the compound and exchanged greetings and pleasantries. One of the men who was hired along with his assistant responded to the greetings. Modiko's mother too happily greeted the old man. At this point the evangelist paused from his work and looked at Rre Tlholego's side to see who was greeting them. He just greeted Rre Tlholego but it was clear that he was just doing for the sake of it. Rre Tlholego then proceeded to his homestead.

"*Monna!* What's wrong with you?" The evangelist barked.

Modiko could not understand the question. If Modiko was not scared of him he could have asked him back for clarity. He noticed that his father's lips were shaking like the thighs of a dog that was defecating on wet grass. He just looked at his father and allowed him to continue talking.

"Are you deaf? I have asked you why didn't you spend time at home anymore? When do you intend to be given tasks to do for me?" He wore an even more serious face than before.

Modiko told him that his grandfather had asked him to help him find some missing cattle. He could feel a sharp pain ripping through his heart because he knew that he was telling a lie. He always remembers the first lies that he told after his baptism. He was required to gather all the goats for milking every day after school. The milk was used for preparing tea. Whenever the goats got lost his father would smack him as if he had spent the whole day looking after them. One day, when after school he went for the goats, he struck the one with black and white marks with a stone because it was going astray. The goat then started limping from a fracture that it had sustained. He took a very long time before he disclosed to his father that one of the goats had broken its legs. After a few days his father saw it while Modiko was still at school. He instructed that it should be killed. Those who slaughtered it found that the goat had a broken bone, almost detached from its flesh like a clay cow. When Modiko came back from school was asked who hurt the goat he denied and said it wasn't him. His father beat him anyway.

Now he found himself lying again because he knows that there is a *kubu* that is always buried somewhere in the compost heap waiting for him in case he misbehaves. He was very scared of his father. He would rather have Senwamoro and the chief rip off his skin with a whip than his father. Hell would definitely break loose if he could confess to his father that he had touched the herbs from the sinners.

"I will only spare you the rod today because of this man," His father said while pointing to the man who was working on the house. "But I am still not finished with you. I am going to beat you thoroughly."

Upon hearing this, Modiko went to the back of the house and sobbed uncontrollably. He did not cry out loud for he feared being heard. He wondered why he did not live life that many other children enjoyed. He has tried all his best to be a good child but that does not help in any way. If he breaks the curfew he knows that he would be punished. He was not allowed to play with other children in the street. He was not even allowed to tell folktales because his father wanted him to read the bible only. He is just like a cow that is only kept and maintained for its use. He thought that he wouldn't be sent for herding cattle after his baptism but that didn't happen either. Ironically, at church his father was such a righteous man and was someone who could cause women to weep when he preached. At home he was different. He was such a heartless bully. Really, what is this thing called Christianity? Such a beast like his own father calls himself a Christian really? Could this be a *botlhodi*, or a bad omen of a head louse that Rre Tlholego talked about?

Chapter 13

At the end of the church service, pastor Mmolaaditso announced that all men in the congregation must remain behind. Therefore, when the women dispersed, all the men gathered under the church's *mhawa* tree. They removed their hats and put them on their knees, while some of them placed them on top of the nearby stones. They kept themselves busy with some casual conversations while waiting for the pastor to arrive. As they waited, the pastor was in deep conversation with other two evangelists.

Mmolaaditso came as if he was in a parade. Oversized and protruding belly of course. His cheeks looked as if they were swollen. "Let there be peace unto you children of God." He said while taking a seat on one of the stones they had reserved for him.

"Amen!" All the men greeted back in oneness like toads.

"Men of God, I will not take a long time speaking, like a man who is working on his garden. I have just a few words. The first thing I want to tell you is about the reports that I have recently received. I have heard that the chief has not left us alone. He is still yet to send his men to take us to prison. The only reason why he has not acted yet is because he is waiting for *letsema* to pass first. He believes that if our hearts and those of people who are feeling pity for us are hurt and heavy the ancestors will not make rain for us. So, his silence is only short lived, like the beam of moonlight in the sky. After *letsema* he will come back for us." He paused for a while and pulled up his tight pants. He breathed heavily. The stone that he was sitting on was not comfortable and therefore he couldn't breathe properly because of his huge belly.

"I thought to myself and therefore wanted to ask you if it could be a good idea for us to register this church under the white man so that he oversees it like in Ramolaisi's church. We are only being persecuted because our church does not have a white person as a member. Because of this they claim that our church is not legitimate, it is unfashionable since it is constituted of Batswana only. They say it was

117

not introduced here by a white man. What is it that a Motswana can do? They ask. A typical Motswana with unkempt hair. So, after thinking about this, I was seriously considering that we appoint a white man as the leader of our church, and in addition give it an English name like Ramolaisi's?"

"Pastor are you done talking? I personally thought that...."

The pastor cut him short by and said, "Just wait first. I haven't finished yet. I want to say everything first and then we can talk about each point separately. It is important that we run the church services very well."

"You well know that money is important for us to run this church. For a while we have been tithing four shillings. I would like to raise it just a little bit to ten shillings per person. This is very important for us to ensure the smooth operation of our church events. As you can see, I am almost naked wearing torn clothes right now. This congregation does not take care of me at all. Other churches, like Ramolaisi's church, are fed and maintained by the congregants. They have even bought themselves very nice cars and that fuel is paid for by the church. As for me I'm in need, I don't have proper clothing and I am starving. My home is now looking worn out. Before I forget, I would like to ask women of this congregation to come to my house for plastering the wall of my homestead next week Thursday.

And finally, before I take much of your time because I know that you are all starving, I thought I should tell you something important. There is someone in this church who is trying to take my position as a pastor. I am like Saul and I am the chosen one. I was appointed as a pastor by Pastor Lefoko who introduced this church here in Molepolole after his stay in Gauteng. He is the one who appointed me. Bamosotla was there, Mojanku too was there and both of them can be my witnesses. If anything, we can go to war fighting for this. That person who is trying to take my position, I left him having gone to fight during the world war for my land. As for him he was just enjoying the tithes and not doing much for the church. Is that what good shepherding is about? When you ask someone to take care of the flock and then he behaves like an owl on chickens? He told the small congregations in Thamaga, Kopong, Mogoditshane, Kumakwane, gaMoleele, Mmankgodi and ga Metsimabe that he was the only one who was now the pastor. We later heard that he frequented his visits to Gauteng and travelling in first class in the train, enjoying bread stuffed with raisins. He clearly got used to that. After tasting all this, he thought he could be the pastor forever. As we speak, he is now taking his son to one of the secondary schools here. He has been heard boasting that his son is going to be a *bioscope* of this church."

"It's *Bishop* and not *bioscope*, pastor," Evangel Mojanku corrected him. He was one of the evangelists who stood with the pastor in front of the congregation.

The men who had gathered there laughed. One of them then asked, "So...what kind of thing is a bishop?"

"He is the presiding overseer of the church," Evangel Bamosotla explained.

It was not necessary for Pastor Mmolaaditso to mention the name of the person who wanted to take his position. Like it is often said, a name can destroy a family. And besides, many men knew that Evangel Letlotla was the one who was left with the flock when the pastor went to war. In addition, he was the only one in that church who was taking his son to Kgari Sechele.

"In this church," the pastor continued after the men stopped laughing, "we don't want the educated people. Those people are crooks. As for ourselves we have divine education. For example, we know how to read the bible, how to preach and interpret God's word. But we never went to school. The education and intelligence of this earth will rot right here on this earth. What did Job the man of God say? He said you will die in your cleverness! It not necessary that a bioscope, *kgae!* I mean bishop, should go to school for training. What will he learn there? Just to count coins and then cheat the congregation? Just look at Ramolaisi, he drives an expensive car."

The pastor stopped talking, almost as if he realized that he had been talking too much and the men were losing interest. He quickly noticed that Modiko was sitting among the men who had remained behind. He just died inside, just like a tuber that gets devoured by a rat.

The evangelist who was interrupted earlier then said, "I personally think that this is a very heavy discussion. The words are quite heavy like a bag of salt. This is where the weight is: there is a lot that has been said. A lot! We don't even know where to begin or finish. But my question is, how will we speak to the white man since none of us can speak English and still we don't want the educated people? That's my point." He closed his eyes while looking at the side where the pastor was standing.

"*Bagaetsho* if at all you would listen to me," Evangel Bamosotla interjected before the pastor could speak. "We should take this matter before the church. The words are so big such that they can't even fit into my ears. We are starving because we have spent almost the whole day here, so clearly, there is nothing much that we can say. The way I see this, I think we have only been told part of the truth. It seems to me that this matter has been sitting there for a while. Therefore, I would like to suggest that, pastor, please give us time to think about these words. I also want these words to be said before him, so that he can answer for himself. Let's just cut it short like that and avoid behaving as if we are praying for rain."

All the men agreed with Evangel Bamosotla even though the pastor was adamant that they should just go ahead with the talk. They also agreed unanimously that this matter be brought in front of the church, and that it was better for them to talk eye to eye, like two African wild cats. Clearly, the pastor did not like this arrangement at all because he wanted to get ahead of evangel Letlotla who at the time was on a preaching assignment in Kopong.

****

Rre Tlholego likes to say that *mogopolo o farasa dikhukhwane*. When he says that he is referring to a situation when a person starts questioning and becoming skeptical about things that he used to believe in. Modiko's mind started doing exactly that. Every morning he carried his books in a metal container and went to school at Kgari Sechele. He walked barefooted to Morwa where the school was built.

During winter the pain of the rocks that he keeps stepping on becomes very unbearable. When that happens, his feet lacerate at times with blood coming from the wound. His toenails are almost finished because of the stones on the ground that he keeps stumbling on.

Most of the time some boys and girls have ceaselessly reminded him he was supposed to wear shoes when he goes to a secondary school. It was not a good thing that he had turned his own feet into shoes. They had also reminded him that he wears the same pants for the whole year.

"Your father is so rich and his house has a corrugated iron rooftop, why is it that he can't buy you school shoes?" One of the boys asked during one of the days at school.

Modiko knew very well that what this boy was saying was true. He decided to keep quiet instead. Then, someone like Evangel Letlotla was regarded as a very rich man. He had so many cattle. When they went for drinking water at the Matlagatshe well, which he owned, they could drink from morning till sunset. One day Modiko's mother told his brother that, "I have not been lucky in this marriage. The only time when we eat beef is when we go to a funeral."

Modiko decided that he would go to school until form five. He thought that by the time he had his own job he would buy himself very nice clothes and shoes. He never forgets a proverb which Rre Tlholego liked to use: "a chick that dies is the one that is still unhatched, one that is outside can fare for itself." That was his resolution.

That morning Modiko was just leaning against the wall while other children at school were busy playing. They were very loud. As he kept on thinking about his life, he could barely recognize their noise. He was looking at the football ground where other boys were playing and next to the ground there were two toilets, one for boys and another one for girls. He could not look at the boy's toilet without remembering the first month of the year, when the school had just started. At this moment his mind was harnessing through these thoughts from the beginning of the school year.

All the newcomers had gathered in one place and almost all of them looked very scared. They had isolated themselves from the crowd like new goats that were new to the kraal. As for the other students who had been there for a while, they were doing everything they could to show off and boast. The senior school boys took the male newcomers to the classroom. They were all ordered,

"You all lie face down to be thrashed!" The newcomers were then forced to lie down and walloped on their backs using belts.

There was this other certain boy who came to Modiko. A giant who looked very scary.

"Hey! Newcomer come here right now. Where are you looking at? I am talking to you,"

He roared while looking at Modiko. In response Modiko came close to him like an ox that is scared of being tied for ploughing. The gigantic boy then stepped on Modiko's left foot using his shoe.

"*Mosela,* you are a car okay, so when I step on you very hard you have to make some noise."

"Rrrumm! RRRRUUUMMM," Modiko imitated the sound of an accelerating car.

The bully then pressed his nose using his thumb. Whenever Modiko failed to do what the senior boy wanted he would give him a very hot slap on the cheek.

"What's wrong with this lorry? Honk and say pe!pe!"

Modiko could not hold back his tears. He cried like a baby. Little did he know that he was inviting even more trouble for himself. All the girls and boys had gathered and surrounded him when they heard him imitating a car. The big guy just instructed once and one of the girls came holding some milk. This was powdered milk mixed with dirty water from the street. So, the milke was reddish in color because of the soil where the water was drawn from. The girl poured some of the milk in a baby bottle which had a teat.

"A baby is crying. Baby drink some milk!" One of the girls said this while bringing the bottle to Modiko's mouth. When Modiko refused, someone kicked him very hard on his buttocks and that's when he realized he did not have any choice. He drank all the milk quickly.

After that they took out a container that was filled with snuff. The big boy gave him to sniff. That day Modiko realized that he had sniffed the snuff that Pastor Mmolaaditso had told him was sinful. To comfort himself, he thought to that it was better that he was forced into doing this and not according to his will. He sneezed heavily until the tears splashed out of his eyes. The boy who gave him the snuff tried to beat him up for sneezing but that couldn't help anyway. He sneezed harder. As he sneezed the girls shouted, *thuthuga!* An expression that is usually said to a baby when sneezing.

It was very irritating for Modiko to see such young girls say that to him but there was not much that Modiko could do. When you see a rock rabbit playing by the tree in your presence, it is a clear indication that its mother is somewhere nearby. So, there was more that Modiko was still to encounter on that day.

"*Hee* Mosela, kiss that woman," The boy instructed Modiko while pointing to one of the beautiful girls.

He felt as if he was swallowing some boiling saliva in his anger. He pretended as if he didn't hear what he had been asked to do, but once again the other boy kicked him. He came close to him and slapped him very hard on his face.

"Are you deaf *monna*? We are telling you to kiss this girl. Your shirt looks like you have just come from milking horses. Kiss her now. What's wrong with you *mosela*?" the senior boy barked.

At that moment, Modiko came closer to that beautiful young girl. She was a very beautiful girl, that even any talented praise-poet would easily run short of the proper words to describe her looks. The girl stood still as if she was ready and similarly wanting Modiko to take an immediate action. A spark of new emotions entered Modiko and harnessed his mind quite vigorously.

Modiko felt numb. And, out of this numbness he felt like black ants were crawling on his back. He came closer to the girl the same way a chicken would come closer to a scorpion. He lifted his neck and licked his lips as if he were preparing to enjoy a sweet delicacy. He tried to kiss the girl on the neck but when he did that all the boys and girls came to him. They poured on him some dirty water and started shouting.

"Oh! Come and see! *Mosela* has kissed a girl."

After that they beat Modiko until he was barely recognizable. At that point, all the newcomers were instructed to form a line. After they complied and queued up, one of the senior boys stood upfront. He was holding a metal container with some dirty water and a dead lizard on the other hand. He stood under the tree which had a bird nest and an ox horn. The senior shouted out the instructions immediately.

"I'm a pastor and these two over here are deacons. Now we are going to baptize you as a way of giving you a proper welcome to this school. After I say something and before I baptize you must say *Yes Pastor!*"

"Am I clear *mesela?*"

The service began. The deacons asked the newcomers what they were coming to do at school. It appears that a certain one had not yet been admitted to school because this was his answer,

"I've come to find out if there is an opening."

Little did he know that he had opened a can of worms. They pulled him out like a chicken being pulled out of the branches and immediately dragged him to the toilet. When they got there, they showed him the toilet hole and said. Here it is, the 'opening' that you came looking for. The poor student tried to look them in the eyes clearly not knowing how to respond. But after one of the old boys gave him a proper hot slap on the face, he complied. When he came out he didn't only look dirty, he was a real skunk. They all left him alone and disappeared.

The baptism continued just like that. Most of them passed until it was Modiko's turn. The 'pastor' then began the service in a new style.

Pastor: "This boy here drinks alcohol."

Modiko: "Yes pastor."

Pastor: "This boy smokes"

Modiko: "Yes pastor"

Pastor: "This boy likes girls."

Modiko: "Pastor, yes."

The 'deacons' approached him with kicks and ordered him to talk properly and politely. He did not have much choice but to comply.

"In the name of King Lizard, *Serotelakgarikgari*, millipedes and centipedes, I baptize this boy." As he spoke, he poured dirty water on Modiko's head leaving his khaki shirt wet. After that they told him that he was a dog and then ordered him to bark at the bird nest that was hanging from the tree. As he imitated a barking dog, some of them beat him claiming that they were now chasing a dog because it was making a lot of noise for them. One of the teachers, big and pot-bellied like a corn cricket passed and laughed his lungs out.

Modiko came back from his daydream when Dineo shook his shoulder. Dineo is that beautiful girl who got him in trouble when he tried to kiss her.

"Modiko why are you not playing? Look, all other children are playing. The church has really turned you into an old man in your boyhood days," Dineo said, after which she pat him on the shoulder and then ran away.

Modiko watched Dineo as she went to the toilet. Going to the toilet does not suit her at all. Modiko thought to himself. He tried to ignore the feelings that were now harnessing his mind. Having feelings for girls was considered a sin, but they were also taught that you must love your neighbor the way you love yourself. He looked the other side. The school bell rang and they all went to the classrooms.

****

"I don't have much to say evangel. I just wanted to tell you beforehand so that you are prepared."

Evangel Bamosotla said while standing up.

"I'm very happy my brother. A good hunt is one where an animal is captured at the end of the day, but that of a human is never a guaranteed success."

Evangel Letlotla remarked while shaking his hand with Bamosotla.

"I will keep my eyes open and will hear the news on Sunday. You will be shocked. Some of our pastors think that the church is some form of inheritance. He thinks that this church will be led by his son.

These days it is better for the church to be led by the educated, so that where we can't manage, they fill in for us."

"Anyways, remain with God, servant of God."

Evangel Bamosotla disappeared into darkness. His fellow Evangelist, Bamosotla, thought deeply about his words and looked at Modiko. If only he could listen, the church will enter into the hands of a good and progressive leadership. The church needs leadership that thinks about the future. The evangelist thought about this and remembered how he once encouraged him to study hard so he could go to America to train as a bishop. At the time, Modiko happily agreed that he will go to overseas, a place that the conscripts never stopped talking about.

"America is not like Africa. Black people there are the leaders," Rre Mokgaodi once said. "Black people are the ones who created the flying machines that destroyed Hitler of Germany. We were with them during the war. They speak English through their noses. The bomb that they created left a very huge pit when it exploded. A kind of pit that could take about hundred men to dig in a hundred days."

That was the kind of America that Modiko was thinking about when he agreed to become a bishop. But as he progressed with his studies he was told a different story from that told by the men who went to fight during world war. His standard six teacher told him that in America black people were suffering like everywhere.

He told them that blacks left Africa chained in their legs and hands and they were held captive as slaves. Most of them died in the sea and they were thrown into the sea by very same people who claimed were Christians. These slaves were used in the sugar and tea and banana plantations. Some of them died in these plantations. The teacher finished by saying that those who are following the religion of slave owners are like slaves of heart and spirit.

Three Sundays had passed, and the church service was led by Pastor Mmolaaditso alone. Normally, something like that was not supposed to happen, when it is only one person holding the services without sharing with others. As a result, almost everyone in the church was wondering what was happening, it seemed as if now evangel

Letlotla was forcefully removed from his teaching privileges. That idea of having a white leader in the church was put aside momentarily. The pastor was sitting on it. There were rumors that circulated saying that the church was getting divided because of this issue. Gossip too became rampant, with some people claiming that the pastor was not getting ready to go to Thamaga where he was going to meet his ngaka Mogatla wa Phepheng.

"He even has a *ngaka*?" Modiko asked.

"My boy, you are still a child. Never get fooled by someone who suggests that using traditional medicine is a sin. *Modi* is our tradition," Ramarepetla responded. He is the one who got demoted after denying them right in front of the chief the other time.

Evangel Letlotla swore that he was going to just say things as they are. Truly after a prayer and when people were about to disperse he opened up and removed a thump that was blocking his throat. He said, "Excuse me everyone, may I aske you all to sit down. I have an announcement that I wish to make."

The congregation sat down and some women were heard complaining. Before they finished he spoke: "Brothers, I am not the one who likes to smear an ulcer with fat. When it gets worse I prick it at once so that it oozes out the pus. Here is my complaint, there is an issue that the pastor once told us. He agreed when we suggested that he should say it openly in front of the church. Therefore, what I am asking is that he should say it now, so that we don't wait until people have gone to their fields."

After saying that he sat down. The pastor licked his lips like a *mosenene* snake. He put down both the bible and the hymn book.

Noise erupted and it was unclear whether people agreed or disagreed with what the pastor was saying. That's when the evangelist who said the other time that these words were quite heavy like a bag of salt intervened. He stood very fast from where he was sitting that one could easily think that he must have been bitten by a scorpion. Most of the congregants laughed. After cleaning his nose, he said, "Fellow brothers, if you had listened to me, it would have been much better to talk about this matter right now. Being hungry should be the least of our worries, we all grew up in hunger. All of us are here, including evangel Letlotla whom the pastor's words seem to be pointing his finger at. Let's talk about this matter eye to eye, like wild cats. I really don't like gossiping about another person. So please talk, pastor."

The pastor scratched his belly for a while. He only started talking after belching loudly. He discussed each point separately and emphasized that the tithe should be raised from four shillings to ten shillings per member in order for the church proceedings to run smoothly. He concluded by suggesting that he thought that it was wise for the church to have a Whiteman as their leader so that he can speak to the king on their behalf. That was the only way their church could live peacefully as it is the case in Ramolaisi's church.

After he sat down, that other evangelist who previously emphasized the weight of the pastor's words stood up.

"My pastor, it seems like you haven't said everything that you wanted to say. What about the person whom you left when you went to fight at the war? The one who supposedly squandered all the money and sent his son to school. Why are you leaving that one behind? Don't cut it short, just feel free to say everything that you told us."

"No, I don't think that will be necessary," The pastor said. He could have continued but evangel Bamosotla stood up.

"My pastor, you are our father. I don't want anyone in this church to start thinking that you could be hiding something. Please don't beat around the bush and tell us everything without having to be nagged as if you were a lazy donkey."

The pastor had no choice but to say it even though he was uncomfortable doing so. He told the full story of how evangel Letlotla used the money collected from tithes to buy his cattle and also mentioned how he even collected the money from a branch in Gauteng. Upon hearing all this, evangel Letlotla didn't know where to look so he shoved his hand on his head and looked down. The pastor said everything that he had to say about Letlotla's conduct, leaving him embarrassed. It was clear that he was enjoying it.

After he sat down there was an intensive discussion about everything that he talked about. However, they tackled each point separately. Most people who spoke seemed to agree that it was necessary that the church gets a white leader in order to stop the persecution that they were currently facing. Some suggested that they just had to keep fighting because Jesus had said his followers will be persecuted and that's when they will see heaven. Pastor Mmolaaditso was very happy to see evangel Letlotla, whom he saw as an enemy, very quiet. Because of this he thought that he had won.

The issue of increasing the tithe was agreed upon although it seemed that some members did not indorse the idea. The people who sit in a lower hierarchy are the ones who are basically providing for those in the upper positions. This is just the unofficial written rule of stratification.

Time arrived for the third matter raised to be discussed but at that time people agreed that it was not right that they should be talking about the matter when the culprit was sitting amongst them. Therefore, they suggested that it was better if the evangelist could stand and speak for himself.

Evangel Jeremiah Letlotla stood up. He removed his shaded sunglasses and wiped his glittering eyes with a white piece of cloth. He then placed the bible on a rock from where he had been sitting all this time.

"Let peace be with you, the congregation of the living God."

"Amen." All the congregation responded, a sad response though. He knew very well that he was supposed to take his time to speak so that everything that he says gets understood clearly. He had mastered the human psyche. During his extensive period of preaching, he learned how a human mind worked. Also, from his boyhood he was a very observant person. One of the things that he observed carefully were ants and flies. When a fly sees a bucket full of milk it just jumps in and dies instantly. As for an ant, when it sees ashes it first tests if it is not too hot by crawling aside it first until it crosses through. This time he wanted to imitate the behavior of an ant.

"Children of the living God," He said while standing up and after putting his books down. "I have been accused of three things. The first one is that I have stolen all your money while your father had gone to the war. The second one is that I want to take the position of the pastor. And third, that I am educating my son so that he takes over the leadership of this church."

He knelt down and picked up the bible, opened it and read. He read from the scripture which said anyone who tries to destroy God's temple, that person will be destroyed by God himself. This caused the rest of the congregation to look at him with obvious shock. After reading, he put the scripture aside and then wiped his nose using a handkerchief.

"In the first accusation I say it openly that the Lord is the only one who knows that all the money that I collected during the pastor's absence I gave it all to him having not touched a penny." He knelt again and took out a small exercise book. He then asked someone who could read to do the reading. One of the young girls immediately stood up and took the book. She had some small dimples sitting on her chicks and looked a bit shy. The girl started reading all the names in that book and how much each member contributed. Each person had contributed four shillings. Those who went to school did their own calculations and agreed that across all the years that the pastor was absent all the contributions collected was a total of three hundred and eighty shillings and a few cents.

"Now, to both of you evangels, Bamosotla and Mojanku, what can you say because you saw me when I gave the pastor all the money when he came back from Europe?" He held his waist.

Bamosotla confirmed that indeed the pastor had received and taken the money as calculated. Mojanku looked at the pastor in a way that showed he was affirming. He affirmed everything that Bamosotla said and stated that the pastor had indeed received all the money.

Shame enveloped the pastor. He couldn't even look anywhere but to just look down like a wizard who had been caught. Instantly all eyes from the congregation were on him. He did not know what to do so at this point he was just moving back and forth like a leaf swayed by wind. After that, evangel Letlotla then continued:

"*Bagaetsho,* I will leave that one alone. Let me get to my second accusation. It is said that I want to take the pastor's position and that I am even taking my son to school to make sure that he takes the leadership of this church. Since I joined this church, my job has been to do God's work of preaching and bringing lost souls to Jesus. If anyone has at any point seen me do something that undermined my pastor let him openly say it now. You are my witnesses."

The evangelist waited for some time to allow anyone who had issues with what he said to identify themselves. He then continued, "If at all sending my son to school is way of showing that I want to take his position as a pastor, they it is fair to assume that we are all trying to do the same thing because most of us here have children who go to school. If at all Modiko will be interested in leading the church after he completes his studies that would be much appreciated because we want to have people who can lead this church in the future when we are no more. Future leaders must have a progressive mindset who do not think about filling their bellies only and without doing much to build a place of worship where we can pray. Everything at this church has stopped because we are only working to feed the belly of just one person. Is this what you call good shepherding?"

"And finally, the church is not like a herd of cattle. It cannot be inherited. If Modiko or any other child in this church overseers this church that will be just a continuation of God's work. Right now as we speak, we are being told that the tithe must be raised to ten shillings. Where will that money go? If we keep on doing this the church of the Lord will be disunited. Jehovah will punish us. That's exactly what happened to Saul's kingdom who chose not to listen when he was told not to take anything for himself during the war. He instead decided to take and keep fleshy animals for himself. Before I sit down, let me give you my opinion on one of the issues that was raised. I don't like the idea of appointing a Whiteman as the leader of this church. We are children of Molepolole and all of us are the descendants of the Bakwena. The King of Kweneng is our father. So, there is no way we can go and take a stranger to speak on our behalf with our father. The Whiteman is but a visiting stranger whom we cannot trust to mediate between us and our king. If for example you happen to have a disagreement with your father, you cannot just run and call a stranger to speak to your father. Our Setswana tradition has proper channels of mediating in place, such as for example engaging our uncles when we have a dispute."

After that the evangelist sat down. It was clear that he had disagreed with most of the things that the pastor wanted and most of the speakers that followed seemed to agree with him.

On that Sunday the pastor's wife, Mma Mmolaaditso did not come to church. Therefore, she did not become part of this heated exchange of words. However, she was shocked to find her husband with a long face and in a very bad mood when he arrived at home. His face had shrunken and looked like the buttocks of a pig. She knew that on that day someone would be in a lot of trouble.

"Give me my coat hanging over there," Mmolaaditso vomited his anger and almost spitting words with carelessness.

She brought the jacket and a rod that the pastor liked to carry. The rod was not necessary just that he liked to carry it for showing off. If he is in that mood, any wise person would avoid asking him any questions. Therefore, his wife did not ask him anything about what had happened. She humbly asked her husband to come to the house which he did. When the pastor entered, he found a jug filled with a liquid that looked like ox urine. The kettle from which it was poured had never sat on the fireplace. That drink was also very cold, so that he did not have to cool it off like a normal tea. After he finished the first cup she had already filled up the second one. The pastor hated it when a cup was not filled to the brim. He argued that the reason why whites did not like to fill up their cups was because of their long noses and therefore they feared they would dip their noses into the hot cup of tea if it was too full. He finished drinking his second cup. During that day he was seen waiting for a lift by the roadside.

"Today the anteaters are going to fight using their calluses and definitely not with their claws. It is not necessary to sniff the buttocks of a man who has just defecated," Ramarepetla said upon seeing the pastor waiting beside the road.

Chapter 14

"When two bulls fight, it is the grass that suffers," Rre Tlholego told Modiko. These days he was not feeling well. He complained of blood clots in his veins which in turn caused a severe, piercing pain between his shoulders. He had told on many accounts that he felt that his days of joining his ancestors were fast approaching. Therefore, he wished that Modiko would be there to take care of the clan when that happens. Rre Tlholego was very happy to hear from Modiko about the divisions within Motlhaoetla church; that there were two factions, one led by Pastor Mmolaaditso and another one by his father. These two factions do not see eye to eye. Some of the church members had even quit and did not want anything to do with the church.

"That's why I am giving you an example about the bulls. These two men are now using the members to fight their disputes. They are using you all. During that war between Churchill and Hitler, Churchill was sitting in a comfortable chair in London while Hitler himself was in his big house somewhere in Berlin. There is not even a single bullet that scratched any of them even though they were the owners of this battle. I can see that the same thing will happen again. These men are just going use you in their dispute just because they want to feed their bellies," Rre Tlholego said. He used his finger to pick up a glowing coal and shoved it into his pipe and sent five clouds of smoke to the atmosphere. He then continued.

"When a pair of scissors cuts through a piece of cloth, it is divided into two parts. Part of that cloth does not go along with the direction of the sharp ends of the scissors. Some of the threads are pruned and fall off from the sharp edges. This is the same thing with organizations and groups. When an organization splits, there are some people who are just left in the middle and not taking any side. That's why you see that others have actually left the church. Those ones will start drinking traditional beer. They will also consume and smoke tobacco and do other traditional things just like any other Mokwena. So as for you my child, whose side are you on?" He stacked his pipe into his mouth again. A thick smoke that smelled like burning wet chicken dropping filled the atmosphere forcefully.

"I'm still trying to figure out where the truth is. After assessing the situation that's then I will make a decision," Modiko responded.

****

The divisions in the Motlhaoetla church left the hearts of believers torn like a piece of clothing that had been ruined by a puppy. Three Sundays after the heated dispute most of them stayed at home and stopped going to the hill for prayers. It was very difficult to know who should be trusted and who shouldn't. Gossip among the congregants grew rampant and secrets started coming out. It was as if it was the right time for the believers to expose each other's sins.

The faction that supported evangel Letlotla dismissed the pastor, saying that Mmolaaditso was just a wicked sinner who was not supposed to enter heaven. They said he was a murderer who had slain many people during the British and Hitler's war. Can such a person lead a holy flock? How can an Egyptian lead Israelites to Canaan? And the pastor who secretly drinks beer and consults traditional doctors. He has even used his Thamaga based traditional doctor to protect this church. Even worse, he has acted like a coward by even leaving the church of God and relied on a white man because he was scared of being flogged by the chief. Is it not true that it goes without saying 'a stick can only kill a rat and clearly not a human being?'

As for those who took pastor Mmolaaditso's side they were making some similar accusations against evangel Letlotla. They accused him as someone who was obsessed with power and the status of being a pastor. They claimed that the pastor was right when he said that the evangelist wanted to steal his position. He has only displayed his true colors. They even accused those who supported evangel Letlotla to be only after his wealth. They are like a dog that has been enticed using a bait. They have even stopped praying at the holy tree and they now hold their prayer services at the evangel's house. Could they possibly be drawn to the house by the corrugated iron roofing in that house of his which looks like a mule?

Rumors and gossip reached Modiko. And upon hearing this, something crossed his mind. Faith does not change a human being in any way. A person remains what he is regardless just like ice turns into water when it gets warmer. Is this not exactly what the followers of the Motlhaoetla church are doing? Every Sunday they were admonished not to indulge in passing malicious gossip and slander as well as the use of traditional doctors but it seemed they were doing the exact opposite. It was at that point that Modiko felt he was losing something. However, he was unsure what that could be but he felt that it was something concerning his spirituality. He felt like a child who was told that a person that they had called their mother for many years was not their real mother. This discovery left him paralyzed and shrunk in thought.

Modiko walked through a tiny, sloped road that leads to Morwa when he was called by some woman from a nearby yard.

"Modiko, Modiko! Wait for me over there, child of my pastor," the voice said.

Modiko reawakened from his sleepwalk like someone who had been unconscious. He answered and went to the direction from where he was called. One of the well-respected women from the church greeted him according to the way they often exchanged greetings at church.

"Let peace be unto you Mma."

"Amen," the woman responded while handing the chair over to Modiko.

She asked Modiko if he was coming from school and when he was going to complete his studies. She further asked Modiko how far he was intending to go with the Whiteman's education and wanted to know if this education was not going to make him go crazy. The woman gave Modiko a paper that was her membership of Motlhaoetla church.

"Son of my evangelist, I didn't go to school for a long time. Now I don't know how to speak English, but in this paper I can see it is written in English. Please, my child, read for me and tell me what it says." She looked at Modiko after talking.

"The name of the church written in this paper is United Pentecostal Church and it is presided over by Norman Middleton of Tshwane in Mmamelodi," Modiko explained after reading.

"Now what is the meaning of all these names my son?"

"The first one shows the name of the church which you are a member of. The name of the church means that it is a spiritual church of what was done during the Pentecost. Its leader is Norman Middleton, and unfortunately I cannot explain the name in Setswana."

"*Bakwena!* This lack of education has turned us into victims. We have been closed inside a sac like cats," The woman said angrily.

"Pastor Mmolaaditso told us that it is the English name for Motlhaoetla church. That means we have been put in a different church without our knowledge. We have been stolen quite frankly."

"Yes, that's true, *mme*," Modiko agreed. He then left and headed to his home.

****

The news about the divisions within Motlhaoetla church made Dr. Lovelace extremely happy. That kind of happiness that looks like foam from traditional beer. At church, he shifted the focus of his teachings from the bible. When all this started he always read from the bible, reading about John the Baptist. But now he regarded *himself* as John the Baptist. He was preparing for some bigger power that was to eventually follow. His job was to bring civilization and to shine light in Africa's heart of darkness. The darkness was in part brought about by the small local churches of unserious people who like to play like children. There was no way he could not tell that to the rest of his congregants.

"We have welcomed six women from Motlhaoetla yesterday. What did the bible say? God's congregation will grow." He laughed out loud as he spoke with a very heavy accent of an Englishman speaking in Setswana.

****

"What did our elders say? Didn't they say that *'phomphokwe yo o maithukuto mabe o iphatlha ka lefuka e le la gagwe'*?" The old man said, with only exactly two teeth remaining in his mouth.

"What does he mean by so saying?" The chief asked. He knew very well that there was a lot for him to say.

"Jeremiah and Mmolaadintšwa hate one another."

"You mean Mmolaaditso," the chief corrected him.

"Yes, I mean that one. They are fighting over church money. It seems that Jeremiah is now demanding Mmolaaditso to give him his position as a pastor. That's why the men have now locked their horns." He used his knife to cut a piece of meat for himself and ate it.

"I have heard that their church has even divided. Each one of them has left with their supporters like wild dogs. We saw this coming when they despised our king. Where on earth have they seen the ancestors get poked like that? The ancestors then showed them what they are capable of doing. Now they are intervening on your behalf and making your life much easier even when the dogs were barking at you."

"I am the eternal rock of Kweneng. A hill that sits in Makotsane, a metallic one that cannot be blasted even by a dynamite. At the battle I am a shield that protects one even from thunder and bullets," the King said while looking at the old man.

"What are you saying *Kwena ya Madiba?* You the crocodile of deep waters. The leader of many nations!"

"When I breath into the spread of the sky it starts raining immediately. How then can ordinary people overpower me? I'm not afraid when the puppies come to me barking because when I point at them they now will start barking at each other or even chase after their own tails," the King said, while dropping a bone he had been chewing for sometime. Rre Tlholego looked at him with surprise as he spoke. His two teeth looked like legs of a traditional pot.

Chapter 15

The metallic millipede made a deafening noise like a he-goat that cannot endure pain of a castration anymore. It finally came into a halt and coughed like a tuberculosis patient. It was then that a gigantic man came out of it. His big belly led the way as he walked out. He wore his black and white hat so as to avoid the inclement effect of the wind. He wore a blue shirt and a black tie and pants, all of which had been ironed very well, with obvious patience of whoever did the ironing. He pulled up his trousers such that it left the protruding belly partially concealed. When the train stopped, most passengers has begun leaving the train while some who had been boarding entered it with their luggage and parcels. One of those who came out was this man. Tall and heavy as he was, he stumbled by the stairs and kissed the ground. Boys who sat nearby started making some noise about it.

"Hee! Jita banna! Jerr! Are you trying to pick money from the ground with your lips? It is my first to see an old tsotsi!" The other boy mocked while the rest broke into laughter.

One of the men chased and cursed them with his rod. "You insolent pigs! How can you laugh at your father when he just got injured? You have bad manners." The boys vanished into a nearby thick greenery bush the same way a head lice can disappear into dirty hair. He stood up and dusted off the soil debris from his knees and started walking with the man who helped him to stand up. He looked at the train as it began to take leave and then his new friend before he remarked, "How this thing can actually cough very loudly! No wonder children like to play and say: 'my uncle has been coughing for some time, even today he still coughs'. It is also said that a certain somebody once saw it and said, 'God is coming and this time smoking a pipe'." His friend replied:

"You Bakwena people, you actually have a reputation of doing weird and funny things. Is it not true that one of you people upon seeing a railway once said, Banna! Oh men! this train must have passed here long time back such that its path has hardened." They both laughed.

They went past the thick green bush until they finally arrived at his friend's place. "I think it is better for you to spend a night here Mokwena, otherwise you can go and see the prophet tomorrow, at day." He advised. They knocked at the door and a women who covered her body with a loincloth came out after opening the door. Almost two hours of eating passed. In the following morning, they took a quick face shower and after they helped themselves to porridge the owner of the homestead then said:

"Hee! Baphuting! People, I entertained a stranger last night whom I never asked for his name. If you had beaten and stolen from me what would I tell people the following day?"

"Me too I was worried. My name is Jeremia. I'm the son of a man from Molepolole whose name is Letlotla. And what is your name?" After they did the introductions which were mainly about their ancestors and history they left. They went through the trees and all this time the man kept on showing Evangel Letlotla the names of the clans and their related histories. Just when they were walking towards the isolated territory of Malahapye, this man used his finger to point a little further.

"Can you see that small hill rra?" He asked as he pointed towards the direction of the hill which looked as if it were surrounded by smoke when it had just dawned in December.

"Yes, I can actually see it pretty well," The evangel replied as he wore his spectacles again.

"That's the very place where Pastor Sebabatsane conducts his church service. Now his homestead is on the other side of the hill. If you keep walking along this path, I guess you will be able to find it without any hassles." They shook hands after which the evangel thanked Mongwato man for his good heart since they met at the train station until now. Mongwato replied and told him that two hands are always better than one. They parted ways.

It didn't take him long to identify the place that he had been directed to. He wiped off his sweat using a white piece of cloth and the major road that led to Palapye separated like a tree branch. He kept walking. While still at the shiny gate, he started knocking. Another man who was wearing a white blazer answered. He wore a beard blanket and his hairless head shone with an obvious fact that it had been smeared with too much vaseline. He opened the gate and commanded the Evangel to take off his shoes and leave all his belongings by the gate. He obliged. He noticed a pile of shoes near a red bucket that was filled with some green medicine. He placed his pair of shoes near this pile. While still being attended to at the gate, the evangel noticed that this was a Zion church just by the way of greetings.

The gate keeper, after he closed and padlocked led him to a small thatched house. He left the evangelist outside for quite some time. The evangelist heard the gate keeper mumbling with someone from within the house. Though he tried to listen to what they were saying, he simply lied to himself as he heard nothing. After a while, the gatekeeper came out of the house. "You may come in Mophuting," the gatekeeper said. "Thank you sir," evangel Letlotla said while he bended to pass through the entrance while the gatekeeper went back to the gate. After knocking briefly, a grave male voice welcomed him: "Come in!" It was extremely dark inside this house. The evangel closed his eyes for a while and then opened them to try and identify whoever talked to him. "There is the chair, rra," The same voice repeated itself.

"Where?" He asked while using his hands to find the chair he was being instructed to sit on.

"In the middle of the house." The evangel started searching thoroughly until he found the chair. He sat down after trying to find the direction to which it was facing. Just when he sat down, a striking light shone directly into his eyes. He closed his eyes. Using both of his hands, he unsuccessfully tried to block the light from entering his sight just like in a way an individual does to avoid the sun shine. He was left hopping like a honey badger after being exposed to light from the headlights of a vehicle. He tried to look to the side of the person who had shown him the seat but it was useless as he could not see anything. It was as if his eyes had been lit with a torch.

"Good morning Rra." The same male voice repeated itself, to which he responded, "Who are you and what are you looking for?"

"I'm Letlotla, Jeremia Letlotla. And I come from Molepolole in the Kweneng region. I came here to see Prophet Sebabatsane."

"Do you know him? And why do you want to see him? What is your work?" The deep voice poked again.

Evangel Letlotla elaborated his story, relating on why he had come to see Prophet Sebabatsane. He started with the concerns that his church is experiencing at the hands of the Chief and his Morafe. He also talked about the internal conflict that was going on within the church itself. He told how his life was now in danger because his pastor had even now gone to consult powerful witchdoctor, one who can command a tladi to strike-dead someone even in the cloudless sky. Evangel Letlotla then finished his story by saying: "This is the misery that has befallen me, and thus it is as if I am sitting on top of a snake pit. That's why I want to consult those that Jesus has given the strength to help us defeat forces of darkness."

"I understand you very clearly Mokwena, I can see that you have a problem but this is nothing with Jesus. But one thing that you have to know is that it is not easy to see a prophet like the sun that can be seen by everyone. But because these forces of darkness are following you like death you will be given permission to talk to him. Please pay ten pounds so that you can speak to the prophet."

The evangelist reached for the pocket of his coat and drew out some coins which he started counting. He then gave the money to this hand that came from the night of the dark. A black hand took the money and vanished into thick darkness again. At this point the evangelist was sweating profusely due to the amount of warm light from the torch that had lit his face. Another hand came again, it had a dark object with a protruding cord.

"Wear those things in your head, and put the rounded object in your ears," the manly voice instructed. The evangelist did and he was scared to hold them as if he thought they would bite him. He put them on his ears and heard a very low voice coming out of these objects. It

144

was a slow and soft spoken voice and it was evident whoever was speaking had immense power.

"Your plea has been heard," the voice thundered, and it went on to say, "But you are blessed for you will be comforted." The evangel was given a series of instructions to follow without questioning anything.

Chapter 16

"Just take a good look at him, I don't want you to start thinking that I am just making up stories. You can see him, right?" Pastor Ramarepetla pointed with his finger for Modiko to see. "Right now, he is entering Mogatla-wa Phepheng's compound. That one is not a traditional doctor, he is a wizard! He is capable of killing someone even at daylight, when the sun is just above our foreheads. Monna wee! You must start shaving all the hair in your head, your father is going to get killed, or else you can just advise him to start fighting for his life. As it is often said in our tradition, a chick that dies is the one in a coop, the one that is outside can at least fend for itself," Ramarepetla said as he looked at Modiko with a sensitive eye.

The wooden fence at Mogatla-wa-Phepheng's yard was new. Thick and heavy thumps of mongana tree had been stuck tightly together such that there was not even a space for chickens to invade. Modiko and Ramarepetla hid by moologa tree to see how long Pastor Mmolaaditso was going to stay at the compound of that Mokgatla sorcerer. He was given a chair after a brief greeting. The traditional doctor then asked him to wait until he had finished consulting with the first client to come. He used this as an opportunity to reflect on everything that had happened. Ever since the last gathering of a heated dispute he never slept properly. After he was betrayed by Letlotla he tried to find transport which comes to Thamaga but he didn't succeed until after four days because of the scarcity of vehicles. On the third day, as he was still waiting, he heard rumors that his enemy had been spotted going to the Ngwato area. His sources even told him that he might have gone to Bulawayo to consult with Ndebele traditional practitioners. The thing is this too; the Ndebele and the Ngwato traditional doctors are one and the same thing. As for Bakwena and Bakgatla, they are masters of thunder, whereas Bangwato doctors have a reputation in causing an individual to lose their mind. Their victim usually dies with his teeth cringed like that of a dead dog. The Ndebele's are very good at sending a thokolosi. Because of his weight,

147

the pastor could no longer ride his bicycle but at least he was happy to have found transport that brought him to Thamaga.

Mogatla-wa-Phepheng's compound lies in the western side of Molepolole's main road. It sits next to the hill that is never climbed by anyone because Mogatla-wa-Phepheng has made it seem as if it belonged to him. When a child climbs up this hill to go and have some mmilo wild fruit, he will just disappear and never be seen again. Parents often admonish their children about this hill. This compound has three houses. The first two sit next to each other in the front of the compound. There is another one at the back. As for this house at the back, no one in Botswana has ever opened it except Mogatlawaphepheng himself. He likes to say all the doctors are similar in their approach and they spend most of the time plotting how they can kill each other. Once they face each other, the battle will continue until one pays with their life. However, if he misses an opportunity to kill, the one who was going to get killed is sure to finish his enemy when he wakes up. This is the same thing that a tsotsi would do to another one that tried to kill him. The life of a traditional doctor is an unending war.

It is not a coincidence that Mogatlawaphepheng is so popular. He is a very knowledgeable man who can perceive modi just the same way a herd boy can recognize the pattern of their cattle. He could simply make a person very sick and then admonish that sickness like a parent who reprimands a docile child. As for the thunder, he had it at his fingertips. If you stumbled him when the sun was about to set, he would just point at that sun and tell you that you will never see it setting. He would quickly disappear into the house at the back. And then the clouds would begin to gather in the sky as if they were smoke from the fire that had just been set. Before you know it, the sky will burn with fire and at the end you will be left lying, facing the sky and dead, having been struck by lightning.

A new story was being told in Thamaga that a certain Modise came to complain to Mogatlawaphepheng after he realized that some man was taking his wife. This man, it is said that he was even doing it by force such that it was now very impossible for Modise to command authority under his own roof. "Now what do you want me to do monna?" Mogatlawaphepheng asked. "Doctor, you are the one that speaks to the ancestors. All I want is for the evil to be removed from my house," Modise said with tearful eyes. "You said it well, that you want this evil to be admonished. I will do that for you until you depart to the ancestors. The person responsible for this evil is your wife, so I will reprimand her. If you don't like ting then it is best to break the container where it is fermented," He said. "I'd be more than happy Kgabo. I'd be glad Mokgatla!" Modise thanked him.

After Modise mentioned its color, Mogatlawaphepheng went to the house at the back. A red smoke was briefly spotted before it vanished into the stiffness of the wind. It was followed by the burning smell of a vehicle that needs service badly. When Mogatlawaphepheng returned, he guaranteed Modise that his wife was surely going to regret. She was going to openly confess to him. He then instructed that a black cow should be led to his cattle post in Tlhakodiawa.

As usual Modise's wife got her period at the end of the month. The first week passed. Then the second and the third passed and she was still menstruating. All the toiletries including the soap finished. Modise noticed this but he just kept quiet because he could see that the nonsense in his house was coming to an end. After exactly two months, his wife had lost so much weight that she looked like a rod. She approached her husband and told him about the misery that befell her. Modise simply told her that it was because of her sins and that was none of his business, he did not want to get involved at all. After two days he felt pity and called her. He then proceeded to tell her that all this nonsense she did with another man must stop in his house. She made a promise that it will never ever happen again. After seeing Mogatlawaphepheng again, Modise was glad to see that his wife's periods had now stopped.

It was because of his deep knowledge of the traditional medicine that Mogatlawaphepheng got his name. It is said that there was another doctor who was as powerful as he was. The two were competing fiercely. One day during daylight, Mogatlawaphepheng lost his sight but when the bones were thrown he was told that the person who was bewitching him was Motladiile. Motladiile called himself a black mamba with a green stomach. The mamba that hung loosely from moretologa tree, one that bites the cow and its calf, until it finishes the entire kraal. There was a couple of things which they fought with. Mogatlawaphepheng called the thunder but it didn't do much except withering away a portion of his apprehender's head. In retaliating, Motladiile caused Mogatla-wa-phepheng's legs to get swollen until they looked like a stack of firewood. Again, when the bones were thrown, Motladiile, the green stomach mamba, was deemed responsible for his affliction.

At that very point, Motswagole said to a group of traditional practitioners, "My men, the battle is not only for the fat, even the thinnest of the thin are conquerors." He went further and said, "you are the black mamba that has eaten and finished all the Kgatleng clans. A serpent is the most feared thing, that fact we well know. But there is however one insect that can bite even more painful than all other animals. That insect is a scorpion. It carries fire in its tail. When you block the mouth of the snake, you have basically finished it. But you dare try to do that with a scorpion, you will indeed see the underneath of your mother's feet! I am Mogatlawaphepheng and if you block my mouth, I will not even hesitate to inflame your veins. You must all take shovels and peaks and go to prepare Motladiile grave. Tell him that he must divide his heritage among his children by tomorrow because the second day will not set for him."

During that night of the first day, Mogatlawaphepheng took Motladiile's stools to his doorstep. The following day Motladiile took his own excrement and bewitched it using a whisk, a dark medicine in a small container with a red cowry in it. Before the day could end, Motladiile died like a dog. Since that day, the name Mogatlawaphepheng got to be associated with Motswagole like this. People would say during their casual talk, 'A scorpion and a snake were fighting and the snake used his venom to blind the scorpion. In revenge, the scorpion used the tip of his tail to cause an inflammation to the arteries of the snake'.

150

At this point the person who had been consulting with Mogatlawaphepheng came out of the house and greeted Pastor Mmolaaditso. At the same time, he appeared to be busily shoving something into his pockets. The pastor followed the traditional doctor into a dark room. After about three hours, he left the house smiling. He even shook his hand with the doctor before he left. The doctor looked at the pastor as he walked with his chest out going towards the road that goes to Molepolole where he was going to wait for a lift. As usual, the doctor used his thumb to press his nose and a shot snuff-filled mucus through one of the nostrils.

"Now let's go my boy, you saw with your own eyes. It's not a good thing to stare at something until tears come out of the eyes. There will be fire. You must tell your father to protect himself," Ramarepetla said as they left from the place where they were hiding. They took their bicycles and joined the road that leads to Molepolole in Dinkgwaneng. "Can you now see this my boy, that's why Bakwena say some pastors are wizards. They can see all this. Well let's go, you have to go to school tomorrow." They intensified their speed.

****

That day when Modiko had just came from school he placed his books at the corner of the house, as usual. When he asked his younger sibling where his father was, he told him that his father had gone to see Bamosotla. Modiko wondered what the friendship between his father and Bamosotla was all about since the church broke up.

The main house of Evangel Letlotla is divided using a tiny wall that is intended to separate the kitchen space from a place where people sleep. Pictures of Christ's crucifixion hung on the wall and others showed two separating roads. One led to heaven and another one led to hell. People going to the hellfire were shown doing all sorts of things: some were playing guitars, while some were drinking alcohol and kissing. At the end of the road they were taking there was a glowing red fire with yellowish flame like the color of egg yolk. There were also two black animals and they were pulling a person into the fierce fire.

Those who had taken the road to heaven were shown reading from the bible, passing by the crucified Jesus, and heading to a very beautiful modern place decorated with shining and colorful lights. It was written, with big letters that told of the name of that place in English: "New Jerusalem."

Modiko whined abruptly. He then stopped looking at the picture. He went into his father's bedroom where he saw two of his beds. He looked around the wall which had nothing except a calendar that hung loosely. He bent to see underneath his father's bed and immediately spotted a black object that caught his attention. When he came closer to it he saw an object that looked like a brick from the mold. It had two metallic horns which sat at a distance from one another. One was painted in red, while another one was in blue. Upon shaking it he heard some water inside and was quick to reckon the water had been put inside using holes which were concealed with six lids. He also noticed two white cables protruding from the dark corner of the bed and then pulled them. There were two bulbs, almost about the same size and form as that of an ostrich egg attached at the end of each cable. At the end of the two cables were metallic pins. He placed the first pin in one of the strings to a dark object but nothing happened. When he did the same with the other pin, a striking light shone forth. Its brightness could even conceal tiny ants from the ground where they hid. He jumped at once, terrified for his life.

He wiped the sweat in his face, and came closer again. He put the corded pins aside and noticed yet another metallic object which he did not see before. It had the color of green grass but in form it looked more like a woven small basket. The metallic object looked like a cup but its mouth had been covered using a sieve. It was not the first time Modiko saw this kind of thing. At some point there were some men who came to Tlhakodimajwe's shop and advertised a picture of a bright woman who washes with 'sunlight' soap only. A similar metallic object had been erected at the front of the vehicle and it was used to adjust the voice of the men who was talking into a cup to be louder. Modiko introspected if his father had gone to buy this things in Mahalapye. 'What did he intend to do with these things?' He wondered.

****

Whatever words that Evangel Letlotla told Pastor Mmolaaditso when the church broke down began to make sense. He realized that they were, in fact, very truthful. He had told him that would be left with nothing like a tree during winter after all of its leaves had withered. During the time when the congregation was divided, most of the congregants kept saying that they will rather die with their pastor. However, Evangel Letlotla and Bamosotla only had only a few followers left, perhaps just a handful. Evangel Letlotla's home was chosen as the place of worship. Bamosotla however, comforted his followers by telling them that this is not the first time this has happened. People usually do not like the truth; but lies are short lived. During the time of King David and Saul for example, all the nation of the Israelites followed Saul because he was unjust. As for David, he was only followed by just a few. After some time, all the Israelites came back to David. In this case, Mmolaaditso represents Saul. When the right time arrives, he will be left by his followers just like leaves can do to a tree during the winter season.

It seems like this moment that he was referring to had arrived. Mmolaaditso's congregants began going to Evangel Letlotla's home for worship. He tried to lure the hearts of the followers by using Mogatlawaphepheng witchcraft. This was so that they could just only focus on him alone. All of his efforts proved futile, however. Upon realizing that things have taken another toll, he devised a new plan. Evangel Letlotla was in a casual conversation with Rre Tlholego when the dark rain clouds began to gather swiftly above the rooftops of houses. A red lighting immediately struck and a frightening sound of the thunder permeated the place instantly. The old man's body was left lying lifeless on the ground. People around quaked with fret fear, and almost everyone started crying loudly. A nearby doctor was immediately called to cause the old man to throw out the toads and mud that tladi had forced through his mouth. Meanwhile some were pulling out the old man's tongue because tladi had shoved it through his throat. The first doctor to come to this incident said there was nothing that he could do as the old man had already died. He even removed his shirt to show them the evidence of long scratches in his body. He explained that these were the nails of tladi as it were trying to flee with his corpse to the person who sent it so he could remove some of the organs from the body.

Three days after Rre Tlholego's funeral, boreaitse or traditional practitioners were called. And the dead bones were thrown and all the throwers agreed that this tladi was not at all sent to Rre Tlholego. Tlholego only happened to be on its way at the time. It was supposed to have struck the owner of the place, Evangel Letlotla. It obviously came from someone who reads from the scriptures. Whoever that individual is must be an important figure at the church and he is fighting with Letlotla to get the congregation back. With all the explanations given, it was evident the culprit would be nobody but Pastor Mmolaaditso.

A fortnight passed since this incident took place when the two factions of the congregation agreed to have an assembly together near Kobokwe's cave. Pastor Mmolaaditso had more than once sent some messengers to Evangel Letlotla so they could get reconciled and end the envy between them. In his response, he sent the messages back with no hope when he pointed out that the pastor and his followers are the ones who left Motlhaoetla church. Because of that fact, they are the ones who must come back to the church. However, after a number of requests the two parties came to an agreement that they all must worship together at a hill near the cave of Kobokwe. The reason for this was to pray for peace so that the church of God could come together in harmony and unite.

The venue had been chosen by Evangel Letlotla, for he had the most convincing reasons. Some of the reasons that he gave were that, first of all this place was not a designated venue for neither of the factions of the divided church. It was thus neutral. Secondly, he reasoned, the place was not the land of Bakwena so it was not possible for congregants to conspire. In the early morning of that Saturday, Evangels Letlotla and Bamosotla were the first to come to the place.

They were carrying a heavy object. From beneath the concealment of his blanket, Modiko secretly stalked them with one eye. After they left with their package he stood by the window and watched them as they disappeared into the thick bush of leologa tree. Hurriedly, he wore his short khaki trousers and shirt and then followed them. He stepped on some rocks and avoided stepping on the dried leafs. He began to hear their murmur as he proceeded to watch them over the trees. After walking for quite some time, they stopped. Bamosotla briefly left Modiko's father who at this time appeared to be guarding the object. He returned after a short while. It was already dawning and different birds had even began tweeting. A male baboon screamed terror into Modiko's lungs.

These two men started walking towards the open terrain of Ramogawane so as to avoid meeting anyone who came from Sermarule region. They paced further through the hill until they put down their luggage. They looked at different directions to ensure that no one saw them. Looking towards the end where Modiko hid, Evangel Letlotla yelled, "Who are you? I can see you!" Modiko froze. He wanted to run away but he couldn't with so much fright. Just before he was to give up, his father looked at Bamosotla and told, "it seems like there is no one there." They began unpacking their package, while Modiko was left panting with relief. A metallic object that looked like a tlatlana[5] was taken out and hung at the top of a tree. Bamosotla tightened and hid it on the thick leaves of mmupudu tree and another object that looked like a cup was hid under the rock. Evangel Letlotla hid a black plate between two rocks. When Bamosotla started hanging the bulbs on the branches, Modiko knew it was time for him to leave lest he gets caught hiding. He then started pacing through the thick bush of leologa trees until he finally arrived in the clan of Dikoloing.

It was just when the evening had started when Modiko met with Ramarepetla to relate everything that he saw on that day.

"Just wait and see my boy, you will see things that you have never seen before. I just looked at Mmolaaditso performing his wizardry

---

[5] A weaved traditional basket.

actions at the place where congregation was going to gather. Someone is definitely going to drop, I tell you. I've been just telling you that there are so many ways to getting rich, but the problem is that it is not always the case that people know how to follow the right path."

****

When the sun was just about to set beyond the sand dunes of Kgalagadi, worshipers from both sanctions began pacing towards the rocky terrain of Mmasebonedi and Ramogawane. Some came down through the other bigger road designed for vehicles that passed through the sandy patches. Those who came from the upper region came advancing from the hilly area as they walked to the east in the direction of the bigger cave. The worshippers came through until they filled up the place.

Trees had been chopped down in the place where the worship services were going to be held. The creator has planted all kinds of trees. There were plenty of them such as maologa, masu, letlhajwa and sebabatsane. Near the open terrain is the road that led to Thamaga and the fields of that region. Mokgopeetsane river lay yonder in the eastern side of the road. This is the road that people have to pass while they keep ducking like a snake swaying into patches of grass. It is possible to cross through this path until you arrive at the clan of ga Moleele.

When darkness started to evade the place the acacia trees could only be seen by their canopies because of masses who had gathered. All members of Motlhaoetla had gathered in one place. Even those who had been inactive had come back to repent and start their association with the church. Because the sun had just set, darkness had not evaded the place that much except the dark shadow that came from the effect of the hill.

As the congregants greeted one another, the noise of the conversations engulfed the place. Eventually they focused only on greeting those nearby.

Pastor Mmolaaditso and the Evangel held their hands together. They even laughed together like the friends they used to be.

Mmolaaditso's teeth could be spotted here and there as if they were pillars of an abandoned hut. They started conversing with nearby worshipers and laughed altogether with them. Among that ecstasy on each one of the congregants, there were only two people who looked unhappy. Ramarepetla pulled Modiko from the back. "Come here so that I can show you my boy," He said, after which they went to the corner of the hill. "Because it is often said that smiling white teeth are the ones that kill, what about those green ones of Mmolaaditso?" Ramarepetla inquired.

"I don't know, probably they kill while eating," Modiko responded and they laughed briefly. Ramarepetla noticed simmering tears that had begun to cloud Modiko's eyes. He immediately knew that what had crossed his mind. He remembered how Modiko cried when his grandfather Rre Tlholego was struck by tladi. They moved towards a flat rock but as Modiko tried to sit on that rock Moagi Ramarepetla rebuked him.

"You have to look before you sit down my boy. This is not just a rock but medicine." Ramarepetla remarked while pointing at the stem of the rock. When Modiko looked, he realized that this rock had been written a cross using a dark substance. He looked closer because it was getting too dark to see objects quite clearly. He smelled it. It was the thick stench of soured milk. "Now what is this?"

"My boy this is modi, a root from a tree. It is Mmolaaditso's doings. I told you that he has bewitched this place so that the congregation does not leave him. Motswana was born with modi and will die with it. Are you listening attentively my boy? "

They returned to the congregation. Silence could have continued to evade the place if it was not because of the chirping sounds from some birds and wild animals. After a rather long prayer, as if it was for rain, Pastor Mmolaaditso stood up. He started his sermon by preaching slowly as he normally did. He looked carefully at his congregation as if he was checking what everyone was thinking about. The verse that he read said that anyone who brought destruction to the church, God would annihilate that one. He put the bible aside and his voice cut across every ear. It caused the sound of an axe when it through a

157

watermelon. He sweated profusely as he talked. By the time he concluded, he did mention that the church must unite so that the work of the lord may continue. Just as he finished, Evangel Bamosotla, who all this time had been sitting at the back of the church stood up and disappeared into the bushy trees. The only people who noticed him were Modiko and Ramarepetla. They watched him as he faded into the darkness towards the hillside. They then knew something was about to happen.

After a spiritually uplifting chant, Evangel Letlotla stood up. He removed the sunglasses and replaced them with his reading spectacles as he did all the time. After reading from the bible, he removed his spectacles and put them aside all together with the bible. He started preaching with the soft voice of a screaming baby. He emphasized the importance of the meeting and mentioned that it was not possible for an Israelite to live along with an Egyptian.

"We must keep in mind that, here in Motlhaoetla, we are all children of God through Jesus. So now, I edge anyone who identifies himself with the name of any other church other than Motlhaoetla to come back to the church. This is actually the way I see it as the significance of this gathering, not to eat pork with Egyptians. No. We have a good reputation among the rest of Bakwena as people who have the power to perform miracles!" He pretended as if he tranced just for the sake of emphasizing whatever he had been saying all this time. He started roaring with a tone of a bull from somewhere between the hills. He changed the frequency of the tone of his voice like a thunder from the desert territory.

"For this very night, God will conceal himself to you. The children, the elderly and even the blind shall witness God's power. Tonight, God will speak to each and every one of you while the liars will be exposed and destroyed in the way a hail rain can destroy sorghum. This is the very night that you will be getting to know your real church! Let us pray!"

At length, he called and praised the God of Christians. In his prayer he begged his God to reveal himself to his people on that very night. Just after he said Amen! When everyone was still rubbing their eyes and some dusting off the sand from their knees, instantly a very bright light sparked. One of a kind that could even reveal lice from its hiding spot on a blanket. There was a lot of fear-induced commotion in the church caused out of this unusual incident. Women pulled shawls to conceal their faces. Some cried for they feared that the snake that lived in the rocks was going to feast with them that day. Mmolaaditso tried to look towards the hill side but the amount of brightness almost blinded him. The bright light then went away swiftly leaving the place as dark as it was before. Probably even darker. A deep roaring voice came out of the heart of the hill. Slow and hypnotizing. It left the audience in awe and lethargic panic.

"I am who I am! God the almighty. This is my loyal servant whom you must trust. Motlhaoetla is my church, which I take pride in...Let it be just so!"

The voice permeated through every ear that had come to the gathering. Some worshipers were heard mourning in repentance. They even came closer to Evangel Letlotla and persistently prompted him to pray to the lord and ask for forgiveness on their behalf. It was obvious now who had won the hearts of the followers of Motlhaoetla between these men, even a fool could tell.

Pastor Mmolaaditso realized this and it disgusted him. His face shrunk like a rhino hide while white foam formed on the side of his mouth. He laughed. Then again, he laughed even more loudly. All the eyes looked at him with apparent concern. He stood up and ran away while still laughing like a person who has been bit by a lizard called mmantseane.

Ramarepetla caught glimpse of Modiko and said:

"What did the old man Rre Tlholego tell us? Hee! My boy? A white man has brought us madness. This is the kind of madness that makes us laugh even if there is nothing funny at all. So, what is your stand now my boy? Are you going to do as he asked you or you will continue to be like a bat forever?"

"I will see my brother. I will find myself and my manhood," Modiko replied. "Since last time Dineo can't go out of my heart."

Darkness spread across the breadth of the hills. The sounds of clashing wings of bats and other night creatures took over.

--THE END--

Printed in the United States
By Bookmasters